THE TRUTH ENSLAVED

YD LAMAR

THE TRUTH ENSLAVED

YD LA MAR

This is a work of fiction. Names, characters, places, and incidents either are the product of the author's imagination or are used fictitiously. Any resemblance to actual persons, living or dead, events, or locales is entirely coincidental.

First paperback edition June 2021
Second paperback edition May 2022

Book Cover: Oliviaprodesigns

ACKNOWLEDGMENTS

To my wonderful husband, who never bats an eye when I come up with crazy ideas, but instead just adds to it, making my stories come alive. My children, who tell me every day that they are proud of me.

To my beta readers. You guys are the real MVP. Thank you for sticking with me through the initial phases of my writing journey. All of your feedback has inspired me to better myself and my writing ability. **Lynn**, Dana, Vicky, Maria, Tree, Beth, everyone who responded to my beta request in the dark group, and everyone else who beta read, thank you for bouncing ideas with me. Thank you for continuing to encourage me. Somerset, thank you for your crucial feedback on some of the more intimate scenes. I've learned so much from you.

To all my readers, thank you for giving me the chance. I hope I can continue to make you guys proud.

BLURB

I'm drowning in nightmares.
The secrets buried, the secrets revealed.
The truth enslaved.
How do I claw my way out?
I need to be set free.
The nightmares that haunt my mind are the same ones that keep me sane.
The tyrant king needs to be toppled.
This board game we play must be won.

Will he reach me in time?
Will he be able to save me from myself?

PREFACE

Courtesy warning: This book may contain triggers for some. Triggers include but are not limited to non-con, unrequited family love, family love, dub-con, depression, violence, torture, abuse of power, neglect, monster cannibalism, choking, biting, blood play, themes of war, liquid restraint and physical restraint, themes that may be disturbing to some readers.

PRONOUNCIATIONS

ERICE: Air-Reese
ISRA: Is-ra
GIARSH: Gee-arsh
RUSPIN: Roo-spin
DROSK: Draw-sk
BONARD: Bo-nard
REWSK: Roo-sk
WORREX: Wore-ex
DEFUR: D'fur
KHEZ: Kez
LADIR: La-deer

To the ones who have lost themselves in their nightmares,
but continued to stay strong enough to claw their way out.

CHAPTER ONE

KINSEY

Reflections.

Is it a mirror? It's wavering.

What I thought was me stretches and the skin starts to string and break apart like melted cheese. The muscles underneath are ripping a strand at a time, the tendons a stark white against the red.

Fangs. Rows of them. Elongate before my very eyes.

One of the eyeballs pops out of the socket and dangles in the air. I'm caught off guard staring at it, swinging like a damn pendulum when the creature before me lunges right at me.

I scream, shielding my face as I land on my ass. The ground is hard as a rock and the pain shoots up my spine, but the pounding of my heart is distracting me.

The tinkling sound of glass shattering pierces my ears as I let out another scream. My body moves in automatic movements, hands against the ground beneath me as it tries to crab walk backward to get away, inadvertently leaving my eyes open and unshielded.

I look up to find empty space. The mirror is gone. I take another look around, only to see my reflection in shards scattered on the ground all around me, but the creature is nowhere to be seen. Eyes everywhere, eyes on me.

Thud thud. I'm going fucking crazy. I'm not staying here.

Turning quickly, I start running, moving myself as far away from the position as I can.

Maybe it turns invisible? Maybe it's still after me. *Thud thud, thud thud.*

Fuck, is that the creature's footsteps or is it my heart?

This place looks like a damn barren wasteland. The ground is uneven, looking like an earthquake came through and tore through the ground.

The sky has a weird orange tan cast, enveloping everything under its glow. Smoke billows out of the ground through some of the cracks, making me fear what's beneath me.

I'm barefoot. I realize this when I step on something sharp, making me hiss and limp.

But I can't stop. I need to keep running. I can't let it find me.

I didn't see whatever was on the ground, since my eyes were distracted by something skittering in my periphery. What was that? It feels like my foot hooked under something, maybe a tree root, as I land on my forearms. Fuck. This shit hurts more than landing on my ass, because I think something sharp just pierced my skin.

The warmth of my blood dripping out of the superficial wound brings me back to the present. I turn onto my back, darting my gaze anywhere and everywhere, in case that thing is still chasing me. There's nothing. Nothing but the smoke that continues to rise in sporadic locations in this weird place.

The cry of something screeching comes from above me and I bring one of my arms up to shield the orange glow that encapsulates this place like we're stuck in a snow globe of doom.

What the hell is that?

I don't have time to wonder, since it looks like it's diving right for me. The blood from my forearm chooses that exact moment to drip into one of my eyes, causing a sting as I try to get back on my feet. There's a pain in my right ankle but I have to keep moving! Rubbing my eyes, I move quickly. It's coming for me!

I feel the wind shift behind me just as I jump over a fallen log. Taking a quick peek behind me, my heart is about to jump out of my damn throat. It's almost on me!

Two strange horns adorn the side of its head, jutting out like it's a lobster claw, broken into two pieces, and one ridge horn juts out right in the middle of its head, reminding me of a rhinoceros. My mind tells me it's just odd that in this barren orange wasteland, this creature stands out like a black and white movie with the clammy grey cast skin.

The screech it lets out chills me to the bone as it opens its maws, its gums a dark crimson against the white of its teeth, while it runs after me. It's bipedal, the chest resembling a human but the arms that extend behind it are attached to wings. No, not attached. The arms *are* the wings. It doesn't have fucking hands. Just grey wings attached to its torso and ribcage like its damn skin was pulled taut.

I don't have time to survey its legs because the thigh muscles on this creature are flexing like a beast on a mission: a mission to fucking eat me alive.

I'm preparing myself to jump over the fallen log before me like I'm in a race for the Olympic hurdles when the creature behind me lets out a different kind of scream. A scream of pain. I skid to a halt, right before the log. Seeing as I'm a damn glutton for punishment, I take a quick look back once more, only to see an even uglier and scarier creature fucking devour the grey one. The new guy is red like the fires of hell with a strong brow bone that makes it look like his skin was boiling before it decided to solidify. The rest of his body looks like his skin has been torn, the wings that extend behind him looking pretty much the same. His mouth gapes open like a damn serpent with multiple jaw hinges, opening just wide enough to swallow half of the grey guy's body down to his pelvic bone before bringing his head back for another crunch.

If I was curious about the grey guy's legs, I'm not anymore. It's still standing there, without a torso, inky black blood spurting out from the wound. The bottom portion of his legs, bending backward with a lethal-looking spike that isn't lethal anymore since it doesn't have a brain to control it any longer.

I don't know what's wrong with me as I continue to just stand there, staring with morbid fascination as the legs fall to the ground. The crunching noises come again as the red guy continues to chew on his prize.

Something clamps over my eyes and mouth and drags me back forcefully, making me scream, but the sound doesn't carry over the sound of crunching.

CHAPTER TWO

KINSEY

I awake with a start. What the fuck?

I'm sweaty and the clothes I have on me are sticking to my skin. I feel utterly disgusting. Rubbing my eyes, I look around again to find a fire pit near me; the flames have died down from what it probably once was. Staring at the glowing embers, my mind tries to clear. What the hell just happened? I was watching that red demon thing eat the grey guy when...

I jump to my feet, making my brain a little dizzy from the quick change in position. I look around anyway, despite seeing stars in my vision. Where am I?

There's just this damn fire pit. There aren't any tents. The orange tan haze of the wasteland is still around me, telling me I'm still where it all started...just somewhere else, somewhere away from the red creature.

I bring my hand up to shield my eyes a bit to look overhead in case I see red wings in the distance when something covers my mouth from behind again. I'm thrashing out of fear because I don't know what the hell is going on. I can't see anything! Not again!

The large hand pulls me backward and right when I think I'm going to fall; a hot body is pressed up against me. I'm freaked the fuck out, because I don't want to be eaten alive. Please, please, please.

The voice that rumbles behind me vibrates through my chest. The sound is deep like it's coming from a barrel.

"Where are you from? What were you doing on the Amber Roads?" Through the haze of my fear and erratic heartbeats my mind tells me it's cruelly ironic for a place like this to have such a beautiful name. Amber Roads?

I shake my head vehemently, because I'm still scared out of my mind, and I don't know how to answer. I don't even know where the fuck I am or how I got here.

I feel him lean in closer and brush what I think are his lips against my neck as he says, "I'm going to remove my hand. If you scream, you will be drawing every single Worrex within three miles. Hopefully, you haven't made friends with the last one you encountered as it ate the Defur that was chasing after you."

I'm so lost, my mind is beyond confused, but it tells me that Worrex is the red beast and Defur is the grey guy. I shake my head again because it's not like I can answer with his hand still firmly over my mouth.

I swear he rubs his face against my cheek like a creep before he slowly moves his hand away.

I'm shaking. I'm crying. I'm probably going into a state of shock. What the hell is happening?

The guy behind me locks both of my wrists behind me as

I strain to turn my upper body to look at him. My eyes widen at what I see, and a whimper escapes my lips.

He doesn't have any fucking eyes. It looks like the skin over his bald skull calloused over, then devoured the top half of his head. His broad roman nose and parched-looking lips are all that peeks out. The rest of his body looks humanoid, except for the fact that it looks like some of his muscles grew over themselves in different portions and started to recover his pecs and ribs.

The middle gapes open like it just decided to stop its encapsulation, exposing the raw muscles of his abs. His abs are a dark crimson; I can see every damn striation of muscle, but it isn't bleeding despite it looking like there isn't any skin to cover it. Speaking of skin, his is the color of beef left out too long, blood drained out, and oxidized.

My eyes shoot up to his face as he grins down at me. He towers over my five-foot-five frame, and the shark grin he's giving me makes me feel as small as a mouse in a trap.

"I-I-I'm not going to scream. I p-p-promise. Please let me go."

"Now why would I do that? It's been a while since I've caught something so...precious." He smiles even bigger and I almost pee on myself.

"I don't even know how I got here. W-what are you?" He loosened his hold on my wrist a few moments ago, and I take the opportunity to slip from his grasp and start taking a few steps back, away from him. A breeze blows my long black hair into my face, bringing the smell of dust and I have to jerk my head to get it away while keeping my eyes on him in case he makes a move towards me.

"Try it and see what it makes me do. I'm already anticipating the pounce, little bit. Your fear is driving me with need." That smile again gets even wider and more menacing.

"What do you want from me?" Despite his warning of getting off on a chase, I can't help but continue to take steps back away from him. It's my fight-or-flight response and judging by his body...I don't think I would win a fight against him.

The screech that emits in the skies sounds far away but reminds me of what's out there the last time I was running. What do I do? Do I take my chances out there? Do I stay with him? What does he even intend to do with me?

Fuck, he looks like he's sizing me up for snack time.

My eyes move on their own now that I'm far enough back to inspect his whole body. There are huge looking pustules on his hips and thighs. His crotch looks like an exploded pustule, the hole like a dirty wound that doesn't bleed. It's dark and I can't see anything in it. His calves look like there's a second layer of skin that grew over the skin already there. His shins look like exposed muscles right over the bone. His feet have huge black claws on them, claws as long as my longest finger. It's big enough to sever the skin if he decides to take a swipe at me.

Something slithers behind him, and another whimper escapes my lips. Is that his damn tail? Why does it look like an overgrown tapeworm? It's swishing back and forth, rustling some of the leaves on the ground. What does that mean? Is it like a cat? Is he agitated? I'm afraid to ask.

The next step I take back, I trip over something and with lightning-fast reflexes, the guy before me lunges.

I open my mouth to scream even though he told me it

would attract those red guys, but I can't help it. This place is like fucking hell! A damn nightmare come to life.

My mouth just started to emit a scream when he lands on top of me with all his weight and a black tongue slithers out from his mouth into mine, stopping my scream from making it out of my mouth.

I shut my eyes and feel the tears fall down my face when he gives me one more slow lick inside my mouth before removing his tongue. If his plan was to make me stop screaming, he succeeded because I'm in shock. His tongue moves from my lips and licks up my tears, and I close my mouth to whimper again. I seem to be doing that a lot. I never thought I was a weak person, but these new situations I'm finding myself in are sure turning me into one.

He laughs against my cheek as he rubs his face against mine. I can feel my body shaking in fear. His tail slithers up my legs and I realize I'm in a fucking dress because the tail is touching places it shouldn't right now.

I don't know where I get the nerve, but my voice comes out more authoritative than I would imagine.

"Get off me."

"I happen to like where I am."

"Don't touch me there."

"Where?" His tail continues its travel upwards between my legs, and I snap. My body goes into fight-or-flight and I bring my knee up.

The only problem here is that my knee ends up in his blown-out pustule right between his legs. It doesn't hit any gonads. He groans on top of me and starts to thrust. Ugh. *Eww.* The hole is starting to get wet and slimy, dripping onto my knee, and I let out a sob.

"Now, now precious. It really isn't that bad. I could be a Worrex eating you right now. Though...eating you doesn't sound all too bad, you do taste particularly delicious."

Oh. My. Fucking. God.

"P-p-please. Don't." My teeth are chattering from how badly my body is shaking. Whatever sliver of bravery I harbored earlier is now gone.

"I love the way you say please." He licks my tears one last time before he gets up off me and brings me up to standing with him.

His arms don't drop from me though, as he continues to stand and look at me. He has no eyes, so I don't know how he's doing it. Nothing here makes sense.

"Now, now. I've only just found you. Stop all this shaking. There are plenty of other things I'd rather do than eat you." That isn't reassuring at all, even though he's smiling like it is. In fact, his smile is creeping me out even more.

The slime that's on my knee starts to cool, and it brings my thoughts back to his crotch. It's still oozing. I'm caught in a trance as I watch the cloudy white ooze start to drip from the opening down to his thighs. The track it leaves behind is fucking glistening. It smells of ... sex.

"Precious, my eyes are up here. Unless... You want a closer look? I wouldn't object." That brings my eyes back up quickly. His smile is absolutely feral, and I feel my cheeks heat up. I was just caught looking at his damn crotch.

"Um..."

"That's alright, little bit. You can look whenever you want. I kind of like the attention you give it. Now let's get moving, shall we? Best we don't stay in one place. Creatures tend to start following the scent, bringing other nastier creatures with them."

This makes sense. Where was he going anyway when we crossed paths? "Where are we going?"

"Oh, here and there. The name of the game is staying alive. We can go wherever you want." A wanderer. A vagabond with no destination in mind. What game are we talking about anyway? I need to get back home.

"Are there more of...you out there? O-o-of your kind?"

His laugh makes me jump and my eyes widen. It's booming, and I didn't expect it. My eyes darted back and forth around us in case something heard his laugh and decided we looked like a good lunch. Didn't he just tell me not to scream in case of this exact thing?

"You are precious, aren't you? My kind..." He lets out another chuckle, and my cheeks are heating up again from embarrassment. How was I supposed to ask him?

"Your ignorance is endearing. There isn't much of my kind left. I'm a Rewsk. My kind used to serve the Underlord before we were banished to the Elysian Wastelands."

What the hell, I don't recognize anything he's saying. Rewsk? Underlord? Elysian wastelands? Where the hell am I?

...How did I get here?

"...What's your name?" If we're going to stick together, I need to call him something.

"Why? After kneeing my inserex and rubbing it all over me, you'd think we'd be beyond this point in our relationship." I don't recognize the words but the visual is enough. His crotch pocket and the slime that oozed out. It's disgusting and morbidly fascinating all at once. It shouldn't be.

My thoughts must be showing on my face, because he laughs at me again.

"You are too precious. I think our time together will prove quite entertaining, indeed. My name is Erice."

"I'm Kinsey."

CHAPTER THREE

KINSEY

The trek was horrible. Some areas of this wasteland are hot near the billowing steam, and other places are strangely cold. Everything is a contradiction, and my mind is having a hard time wrapping around things. I'm barefoot, and my feet are not thanking me. I think I'm going to get blisters, but Erice continues to set a brutal pace.

I don't want to be left behind to be eaten, so I catch up as fast as I possibly can without dragging too far behind.

Once we reach a cluster of trees that look like it recently survived a forest fire, Erice starts to gather some hand-sized rocks around us. My assumption is that it's for a fire pit circle.

"Kinsey, our people lived out in the wilderness during the olden days. Being one with nature, that's who we were. Life and change have brought us to the land of the free, but never forget the blood that runs in you."

"Grandma, does the blood make us different? I thought people were just people?"

Her smile makes her face crinkle, and it brings a smile to my own. I love my grandma, and I love her stories.

"It is said that our people are closely related to those from ancient Mongolia. Our blood ties are strong, but we became our own people once we settled in the harsh winters on this side of the world. It's been generations since that time and my mother found herself wed with an American man who brought her to the states from Alaska to start a family."

She has the craziest stories. Sometimes it feels like it can't be real like it must have been some sort of fairytale she makes up. But looking around me at all the different ethnicities surrounding us, can it really be that far-fetched? This place is saturated with history. History that flows through all of us.

Looking around our neighborhood, I watch as the other children from different backgrounds play with each other in the streets. Some parts of this country are known to be a melting pot of different types of people, more so along the coastlines.

"Kinsey, if you ever feel lost and forget who you are, look in the mirror. It is your eyes that give you away, it speaks of a past that cannot be buried."

I take my eyes away from the kids playing in the streets and look over at my grandmother. Her eyes are the most beautiful shade of hazel that is striking even against her sun-weathered skin. Our entire family has different ethnicities married into it, making our bloodline alone a grand 'ol melting pot in itself.

But I know exactly what she is referring to. Despite my, what many would call, mostly northeast Asian features, it's my grey eyes that set me apart. I'm the only one in the immediate family that has it. Grandma always told me that it was a common trait that was lost amongst our family for past generations. Until now. Does that make me special? It really doesn't feel like it.

Sometimes I think it makes me the black sheep of the family.

I must have been standing in the same spot for too long because when I come back to the present, Erice is standing right in front of me with his head tilted to the side.

I must have been crying because my cheeks feel awfully cold in tracks down my face when a breeze comes by. I close my eyes and let the rest freely fall as Erice uses one of his clawed fingers to brush my tears away.

"Come now, little bit. It isn't so bad with me, is it? We've only just started. We will stop for the night and rest up. Tomorrow is a new day."

When my eyes open back up, I see Erice with his shark smile, and I almost want to laugh at the absurdity of everything. How did I get here? More importantly, how the hell do I get back home? I thought Grandma was telling tales. Looking around me now, none of this can be real, can it? Her stories didn't sound real, either. Maybe I am ignorant of the world.

"It is quite peculiar..."

"What is?"

"...to have eyes the color of death." I suck in a breath and take a step back. What the hell?

"Oh, don't take it so harshly now. The wastelands are a much harsher place than my words could ever be. Death sucks the soul out of any living being. With it, it also takes away the color of life. Your eyes remind me of the carcasses left to rot in these parts. It reminds me of home."

I am unsure of how to respond to that. Is it an insult? Is it a compliment? It's so damn morbid. What's even more morbid is that...this fucker doesn't even have eyes, so how can he know this?

Erice smiles again and pulls me by the hand.

"Come now, this part of the wasteland is known to have high winds because of the trees and location. It is better that you and I rest together and conserve our body heat, yes? The fire will only last for so long."

The moment he talks of rest is the moment my body decides to shut down. My legs buckle and the blisters on my feet start to throb. Erice is quick with his reflexes and picks me up bridal style before my knees can even hit the ground.

He places me on a bed of leaves about a couple of feet from the fire and proceeds to lie down behind me. It has been a trying day and I'm more than ready to just shut my eyes and hope I wake up back home.

My eyes are a blur. Too much color all around me. Deep reds and umbers, dark wood, and shadows.

The reflections of lights and the bouncing of sounds drowned out by the racing of my heart. Footsteps, a lot of them. The closer they get, the harder my hand grips the item in my hand. When one of them puts a hand out in front of me, palm out, my voice clams up.

"Everything's going to be okay." Everything is going to be okay...now.

"We're going to have to ask you some questions." I'm not sure I have all the answers. But he promised. All we have is each other. My heart feels content with that fact.

As the adrenaline starts to fall, I feel my body becoming weak. I fall to my knees, right into the pool of blood below me.

A hand is roaming my breast over the thin dress I have

on. It makes me disturbed and hot and bothered all at once, waking me up. What the?

I slap his hands off me and sit up, turning around to glare at Erice, who only smiles back.

"Good morning, precious. Since you're awake, I say we get started on the day, hmm? Let's see if we can find something to satiate our appetites. Though, I can think of other ways to satiate our appetites without having to leave our comfortable position."

Is he propositioning right now? My stomach takes that very moment to emit a loud growl. Erice rolls onto his back and just laughs. How embarrassing.

"What is there to eat around here?" My mind can't even comprehend a chicken in a place like this.

Once his laugh turns into chuckles, Erice puts both of his hands behind his head like he has all the time in the damn world. Maybe he does. But he can't tease me with food and then act like he's just kidding.

"We'll see what kind of creatures we can come by. It is much too early for the more delicious ones. How about you lie back down and we can finish what we started?"

Ugh. I make to stand and look around for a stick big enough to poke our dying fire. Finding one that will fit nicely in my hands, I bend over to pick it up, only to feel Erice right up against my ass. Shit.

"I do enjoy the company you provide, precious. Perhaps we can get to know each other better soon, yes?" The feel of his warm front against my back makes me feel trapped. He's been nice so far, but I don't know if I can trust him yet.

"You know me, Kinsey. You know me..."

The fear that runs down my spine and the confusion in my

mind makes everything feel so convoluted. It doesn't make any sense.

"Just close your eyes, Kinsey..."

The memory hits my mind like a sharp stab, and I quickly turn with the stick in both of my hands. The slight slip of the wood feels like abrasions on my palms, but my mind is too focused on getting rid of the memories.

Erice quickly removes his body and grabs the stick in his hand like I didn't just try to smash his fucking ribs in. The smile that creeps on his lips makes me even more confused.

With one good tug, the branch cuts through my palms as it's pulled out of my grasp and thrown to the ground beside us.

"If that's the way you like it, I would be more than happy to play."

Despite the pain in my hands, I shove him off me and glare at his face.

"We need to keep moving. Let's find that food you promised me." His laugh is maniacal, but he just starts walking past me like nothing weird just happened between us. I follow after him because I *am* hungry, and I'm not going to stay back at camp all alone for something to eat me.

I catch up to Erice and his damn tapeworm tail caresses one of my calves. I shiver because it's the weirdest thing ever. Does it have a mind of its own or is Erice controlling it?

I'm staring at the ground beneath me as we walk uphill, trying to avoid damaging my bare feet any further when my chest hits Erice's arm. Looking up, I see Erice looking ahead with his left arm out to stop my footsteps.

A breeze comes through our path and I smell something foul. It reminds me of a sewer rat. Disgusting.

"I do believe you may be a good luck charm for me. Breakfast is just over this hill." I want to gag because he can't be serious. We're going to eat sewer rat?

His tail taps my ass and, like a flash, he disappears. What the? Where did he go?

I turn around 360 degrees, and the sound of a growl coming from my left catches my attention. Turning to the noise, I see Erice in the air coming down on something. My legs start running uphill before my mind can even consciously tell it what to do. Holy shit.

When I make it to the top of the hill, my heart freezes.

Erice lands a strike on a large hairy beast beneath him with the claws on his feet. Deep maroon blood spurts out, coating Erice's calves as he continues his assault with the claws on his hands. The beast looks like ... fuck; I don't even know. My mind is having a hard time trying to find images to associate with it or anything close to it.

It has a cone-shaped head, with an underbite that reminds me of a damn piranha. The neck skin folds hang down like melting flesh to create some sort of gizzard. Its front arms remind me of a praying mantis or something. The back end of the creature is too short for the size of his front half, its hind legs much too small for it to even be able to move a creature like that. It makes you think the thing drags his back half wherever it goes. The back has some weird protruding spines that have no sort of pattern whatsoever, but it is these protruding spines that Erice stands on.

I'm holding my breath as the thing thrashes like a raging bull, trying to get a swipe at Erice when Erice suddenly bends his torso to wrap one of his arms around the beast's neck.

In one smoothly orchestrated movement, Erice brings the black claws of his other hand straight across the beast's neck, bathing the barren land beneath them in maroon splatters. It's so morbidly fascinating. He rides the dying beast like a damn cowboy as its body hits the ground in a loud crash, bringing vibrations even to where I'm standing. My mind can't stop picturing Erice as a ballet dancer or artist who just created his next masterpiece.

Does that make me crazy? Why was that the most beautiful sight I've ever seen?

My feet lead me again, this time down the hill, and before I can think about it, I'm a few yards away from Erice, who still stands on top of the beast like it's a trophy.

He smiles his shark smile at me, and it doesn't scare me as much as the last time. The dead creature still smells like a sewer rat, but my stomach grumbling tells me it doesn't really care at the moment.

Erice jumps down with a thump, landing on his feet, and does the weirdest thing. He breaks the two front praying mantis claws off the beast, climbs back up, and shoves the sharp end into each of its shoulder blades. He jumps off the beast's back again and runs like the damn Flash towards some of the trees surrounding us. What the hell is he doing? Am I supposed to guard this thing? ... in a damn dress...without any shoes?

My mind didn't have enough time to even wrap itself around the absurdity of the thought when Erice comes back with some mossy looking vines of sorts. Watching his quick movements, Erice fashions something that connects the two mantis claws. Coming around to where I'm standing, he starts to tie part of the vine around my torso. I'm about to ask him what my mind is wondering when he starts to fashion the same tie around his torso. Huh?

"Shall we? If we move now, we may be able to eat in the next hour or so." Uh...

Erice starts walking forward and the moment the vine becomes pulled taught, the momentum of his walk starts to drag one side of the beast along the ground. Oh, that's what he's doing. He just made us sled dogs. Well, okay then.

We both start trekking forward, slowly dragging the beast behind us. This thing is heavy, making me use muscles I haven't worked before. When we make it to another gathering of trees, it becomes harder to drag the beast behind us from the new friction the dead grass brings.

The moment Erice stops to untie the vine is the moment my body falls down, landing on my butt in exertion. This shit better be worth it. I feel like I worked off twenty pounds just to eat something that might taste like ass.

Beggars can't be choosers though. From what I've seen so far in this barren wasteland that looks like a level of hell, there aren't any chickens or sheep around.

I lie on my back on the ground, trying to catch my breath. The bottom of my feet still throbs like a bitch, but my exhaustion overshadows it.

I must have dozed off because my eyes struggle to open back up when I feel someone massaging my feet. When something wet touches it, I jerk my feet back towards my body. What the hell?!

Erice laughs and continues to tongue between my toes. *Fucking hell. Eww.*

"Quit your squirming, I'm just soothing your feet in case

we need to get a move on." Soothing my feet? It looks like he's enjoying it much more than he's letting on. Ugh.

"Now your little toes don't taste as good as your mouth, but I'll take what you'll give me." That stupid smile graces his face again. Disgusting bastard. My face must be showing my emotions again, but Erice just laughs.

I watch as he gets up to grab a skewer of meat off the fire. Damn, how long was I asleep to have him create something to allow him to slow roast and rotate meat over the damn fire?

The closer the smell gets to me, the more my stomach reminds me of how starving I am. Now that it's cooked, it smells kind of like grilled chicken. Erice hands me the wooden skewer and I'm devouring the food like I forgot all manners civilization has taught me.

I continue to chew as I watch Erice lift a waterskin bladder of sorts to his mouth. The first chug he uses to rinse his mouth and spit out. The next gulps going down his throat remind me of how thirsty I am on top of how hungry I am.

Once I swallow the bite in my mouth, I clear my throat before attempting to talk.

"Where did you get that? Is that water?"

Erice smiles wide and shakes the waterskin in front of him.

"This little thing? Well, precious, upon my wanderings to create our lovely fire here I just so happened upon an unsuspecting visitor. He wasn't invited to our party, but his supplies were." Is he saying what I think he's saying? Where is the other guy's body, though?

"If you are curious about the body, you can stop right

now. I chucked his body off the next hill. I'm sure someone else or some other creatures can make use of it. Ashes to ashes and all that." I just keep taking bites out of my food because I just don't fucking know what else to do. This place and its rules are far beyond my comprehension right now. Or maybe it's just Erice. He doesn't seem to follow any sort of rules or moral code.

When I'm done eating, Erice takes it upon himself to help tip the waterskin into my mouth. I just think he wants any excuse to touch me. I narrow my eyes at him as he continues to give me water. He just smiles the way he always does in response to my suspicions.

I'm lying on my side with my back to the fire as I watch the strange muscles on Erice's back flex as he pulls the claws back out of the beast's shoulders. From what's left of the beast, anyway. I only ate a skewer or two of meat, but I swear about 80% of the beast's body has been mauled into. Did Erice even cook his portion? Fuck, he probably eats that shit raw... I mean, look at the last guy. The red guy that started devouring the grey guy. This place...

I must have been dozing off again because when my eyes open back up, the beast's carcass is gone. Where is Erice?

The moment the question crosses my mind is the moment I feel his arm tighten around my waist. His breathing is slow, making me think he must be asleep. The nights in this place are bizarre because there's still a light orange glow in the distance, like the sun refuses to go down all the way.

My eyelids become heavy and the warmth from Erice's body is seducing me into sleep again.

"Kinsey, you're all I have. I'm all you have. We have to stick together. It's just you and me."

He pulls me into his body even tighter as the arm around my waist starts squeezing tighter.

"I don't know what I would do without you. You're all I have..." There's a vulnerability in his soul that speaks to mine.

My heart swells with the love I feel overflowing, its beat thrumming slowly to the beat of his heart behind me. Closing my eyes, I feel the wetness of my pillow beneath me as my tears continue to escape.

CHAPTER FOUR

KINSEY

The next day proves much better than the last. Surprisingly, there are no blisters on my feet. I don't know how I feel about the fact that...I mean; the guy was tonguing my feet yesterday. Did that have anything to do with it? Does his saliva have healing properties or something? Am I thinking too hard about it?

Erice also made me some moccasins. I woke up, and there they were, keeping my toes warm and toasty as my mind started thinking about how my feet weren't hurting anymore. Kind of sweet, I guess? Also kind of creepy because I didn't wake up when he was putting them on me?

The claws that belonged to the beast have now been fashioned into some sort of double sword that Erice now wears behind his back. It reminds me of a samurai in the days of old. It reminds me of my love of reading, which then reminds me that I have no idea where I am or how I will be able to get home. Is Erice going to be my knight in shining armor? I'm still on the fence about whether he's a good guy or a bad guy. But when Erice turns around and gives me his crazy smile, I swallow the thought back down. He is a fucking lunatic. I don't know if I should trust him or keep one eye open in case he decides to eat me.

One thing's for sure, he has some crazy skills with anything he acquires. 'Acquire' being a very loose term. Thinking back on how he fashioned the vines to help us drag our meat to how he 'acquired' the water skin. I'm sure the chest straps he's currently wearing criss-crossed on his chest to house the claws behind him are from the supplies he gathered the other day. I shouldn't even ask about it, no matter how curious I am. It might make waves I'm not prepared to handle. For now, I need to stick with him until I find a way back home.

Getting up from the ground, I stretch the kinks out of my body. Sleeping on the hard ground reminds me of ...

"You and your damn brother can just sleep on the floor. You're fucking lucky I even let you do that."

He holds my hand tightly as our father brings his legs out to kick my brother in the ribs, making him groan in pain.

I shake my head to rid myself of the thoughts. I need to get home.

The moccasins on my feet feel really good, but this damn dress I'm wearing is doing nothing to protect me from the elements. Erice's tail taps my thigh and I bring my eyes back to him. His back is to me as he continues to fiddle with his chest straps. Does his tail have a mind of its own? He's still butt fucking naked, and the billowing steam from the fire he just put out makes me feel like I'm lost in some ethereal realm. *Where am I?*

Erice turns and startles me a bit as he tightens a belt around my waist. What the hell? What is that going to do? What do I need a belt for?

My thoughts must be running across my face again. I've been told I don't have a good poker face.

"Just in case. It's a good thing to have. You'll never know if you might need it. It's not going to hurt you to wear it so wipe that expression off your face, little bit." With another surprise tap on my ass with his tail, Erice turns and starts walking.

I start jogging until I match his pace and we both continue on our way to nowhere.

We cover more ground today, it feels like. It must have something to do with my feet not hurting so much. I guess I should thank Erice for that.

The orange glow to everything has come back since the sun's rising. The billows of smoke coming out of the cracked ground make me think that this is exactly what it would look like if the world ended.

Wait.

Did the world end, and I didn't know about it?

"Erice, where did you come from? Did the world end, and I didn't know about it?"

"Your ignorance is endearing. What are you talking about? The world remains as it always was. It is how you see it now. Nothing has changed. Besides the fact that I found you wandering around. I do not know what your kind is, but you do prove to be quite entertaining in my wanderings." I can never tell if he's being insulting or if he's complimenting.

My kind? A person? A human? Where the fuck am I? With too much time on my hands, my mind flits back to a memory buried deep.

The hammer strikes and I'm whisked away into a world I never would have imagined.

Their eyes are all on me. Scribing. Speaking. Asking.

It overwhelms my sense when the one person who grounds me isn't here to hold me up. The castle walls I've built around myself start to crumble one stone at a time.

It's stifling. Sometimes I feel like the walls are closing in around me. But it happened, right? You can't take it back. Not now.

But I can slap the hand that has a finger sweeping into my mouth, making me want to gag.

We exit the cluster of trees we've been traveling through for the past hour or so. It feels hotter out here in the open, more humid. Is it from the smoke? Staring at the cracked ground beneath my feet as I walk, my long black hair whips into my face. What the?

I look around and see that Erice is sprinting forward without me. Fucking hell? Is he leaving me behind? No. He looks like he's chasing something.

Is the ground pulsating? I run towards the direction he took off to and stop when I see something that blows my mind.

There are a group of...creatures over there fighting something I can't see. The one guy that stands out the most is the one that looks like he's on a horse of sorts. The weapon in his hand looks like a damn giant ax and scythe on steroids as he swings it around, lobbing off the heads of whatever they're fighting.

Blood is gushing and splattering everything in its wake, the wet noises unmistakable. There Erice is, each hand holding a claw and decapitating the humanoid guys from behind. What was once about five is now down to two.

The guy on the horse turns around and... fuck. It's not a horse. That's his damn body! The top is a man? A male? His armor is spiked at the gills and the helmet sports the worst of it. There are also double swords behind his back. His armor goes down his horse body all the way to the start of his tail. He brings his front horse legs up as he attempts to swing his ax down in a wide arc.

Erice is more agile because he's smaller than the horse body. He rolls on the ground and cuts off the legs of the last bipedal guy by the kneecaps. But during his descent, the guy swings his sword towards Erice's chest, squirting some of his blood in the air. It's macabre.

The horse guy brings his axe to the ground, missing Erice by mere feet. Erice, acting like he didn't just get his chest cavity sliced, rolls on the ground again and jumps back onto his feet, still holding his weapon with both hands.

My feet start walking forward now that the battle has come down to one on one. What do I do? How do I help Erice? Fuck!

The horse guy lowers his two front legs and brings his hind end around for a back kick right into Erice's wound. Erice flies back and hits a boulder with a loud crash that makes me wince.

"Nooo!"

Shit, did I say that? Shit, now the horse guy's attention is on me. The swing of his horned helmet comes up sharply as he starts running towards my direction, the sound of hoof-beats beating on the ground mimicking the sound of my heart beating out of my chest. The metal on metal grates my very nerves as I continue to run as fast as my legs can carry me.

I don't know where I'm going, I just know I'm getting the hell out of here. The trees! I need to get to the trees to give me more coverage. This fucker coming after me is huge, that'll slow him down.

The sound of a pained whinny floats in the air and goddamnit, it makes me turn around. Erice is on the horse's back with his double weapon across the torso of the horse guy. But the horse guy, having the advantage of a higher torso, turns, causing Erice's weapon to spark against his metal armor. He removes one of the swords from his back and swings it at his opponent on top of him.

Erice jumps off the horse guy's back right before the blade can kiss his legs, landing on the ground beside them. He kicks out a foot sweep, but the horse guy rears up on his hind leg and swings his ax straight down, knocking Erice onto his back. The blade of the axe landed right by his head, cutting into part of his shoulder. Blood is freely oozing, but not a sound comes out of him. Is he dead? Shit. The copper smell of his blood carries in the wind.

I'm scared shitless and my brain is in a fog because what the hell am I supposed to do now? Erice was the one basically keeping me alive. Shit, this is it. This is where I die.

That was the last thought that crossed my mind right before the horse guy lunges for me.

CHAPTER FIVE

KINSEY

The wind picks up, and the skirt of my dress starts to fly up. I quickly push it back down with my hands, bending over a little bit to keep it down. Thank goodness it was just a short breeze. Maybe wearing a dress was a bad idea today?

"Kinsey, let me help you!" David's voice comes from behind me. I turn around just as he comes up to block my back, in case the wind blows my dress up again. I feel my face turning red just thinking that he might have seen my panties.

His hands slowly push down my dress from between us, caressing over my butt and back of my thighs. Is this happening right now? Is he just being helpful?

"We can't be together," I whisper under my breath.

"Why not?"

I don't have time to decide what his actual intentions are when his body is pulled off me. I turn around quickly to find Waylon on top of David, throwing his fists in his face with loud thuds, making me horrified.

"Get your hands off my sister!"

David sneaks in some sort of move that allows him to roll around with Waylon as they continue to thrash and punch while my heart beats out of my chest, unsure of how to stop the fight.

I start to wake up, but my head is pounding. When I go to rub my eyes, the sound of chains rattling nearby making me open my eyes wider before I reach my goal.

"Hey, precious. Welcome back." Erice coughs up some blood and the horse guy shoves the smaller blade end of his ax under Erice's chin.

"Silence, Rewsk. I did not give you permission to speak. You should be happy I give you permission to breathe."

"Touchy, isn't he?" The flat end of the blade slaps Erice in the face, knocking him onto his back.

I suck in a breath and turn to look at the horse guy in case he's going to hit me too. I can't really see his face; his large helmet is in the way. That makes him even scarier. Now that I'm close enough, his helmet looks like a damn blade in itself right in the middle, simulating a mohawk. It sits between the two large minotaur-like horns that also jut out of the sides. You can impale a torso on that thing and see it come out the other side. The chest and shoulder armor is plated in sections allowing him movement. Spikes are poking outward from the horse's chest area under his torso. I wouldn't be able to get close to him even if I wanted to. There are spikes on his back too, but it's much shorter and smaller, less lethal-looking versus all the other spikes jutting out of him. He is a walking weapon with or without the giant ax.

His eyes are glowing red, casting such a contrast against his black pupils that look like it's boring into your soul the longer he stares at you. Which is exactly what he's doing at this very moment. Erice is still coughing up a lung next to me, but I can't look away from this new guy. What if this is some sort of predatory challenge? What happens when I look away? Is he going to eat me?

"What are you?"

I take a gulp because his voice sounds like the drums of a thousand death rattles.

The blood splatters the walls, my hands, all over my face. The warmth of it cooling quickly with each breath I take.

The longer I cry, the more I notice the contrast in temperature between the two. The cooling blood. The warm tears flowing down my face.

My hand is holding something. I'm in a zone. Blinking a few times, I hear my brother Waylon growl. *Turning to my right, I watch as the blood drips from his chin and I can't help but feel so calm...so relieved.*

I'm still staring into his eyes as the body beneath us lets out a crackling, wet breath one last time before everything falls quiet around us.

"Female. Answer me when you are spoken to." I jerk back, the memory fleeing from my mind.

"I-I-I'm a person. I mean, a human. A human female."

The guy in front of me stares at me for a few more seconds before he bends his front legs down to the ground in front of me, bringing his humanlike torso closer. One of his human arms reaches out to grab me by the belt around my waist to pull me closer.

My head tilts back really far, just so I can look at his face and not break eye contact. This close, I can see him much better now. I can see the bottom half of his face, which looks like someone ripped his skin right off his face and all that's left is some muscle strands across a skull bone. My mind tells me he's humanoid on top, but the exposed dentures are so sharp, I know it's not the truth. Is anything normal here?

I can't tell if he's smiling or frowning, but his eyes flicker. Or is it a mirage?

"You two will be escorted to the Underlord's keep." Why does that send shivers down my spine? Didn't Erice mention something about an Underlord when I first met him? Is he like a King?

Erice is coughing and laughing at his statement. Does he have a death wish?

"What use am I to the Underlord? That creature who sits upon his throne has all but eliminated my kind after he 'allowed us to leave' his divine presence. He can rot in hell for all I care." I stifle my gasp. Are those fighting words? Dammit, Erice!

Horse guy quickly gets back up on his front feet, rearing back and pressing one onto Erice's chest, pinning him to the ground with his weight. I don't know if I should keep hanging around him. He obviously doesn't care whether he lives or dies. This fucker might drag me with him.

...And he calls me ignorant.

"Do you serve this Underlord, then?" I need to find out all the information I can. Maybe it'll help me escape. I need to get his attention off Erice and his stupidity.

"Do not try your tricks on me, creature. Your fair skin may fool this stupid thing under my hoof, but you will not fool me. I am the Underlord's knight for a reason." There we go. He was bound to slip up somewhere. So, he's a knight, huh? Like a knight from hell.

"So, um... What is your name? I don't want to call you

'guy' and offend you or something. I mean, since we'll be stuck together for a while until we reach the Underlord's keep and all." Damn, he's a monster, and he's the knight to someone. What does this Underlord look like? I'm afraid to find out.

The horse guy removes his foreleg from Erice's chest, but not without one more kick to it, knocking the wind out of him, making him groan. Geez.

"I am Giarsh. You will be marching under my orders until we reach our destination." Damn, even his name sounds like a douche. Okay then.

Erice brings both of his hands behind his head and continues to just lay there like we're on a damn vacation and he didn't just get kicked by a horse. The fuck?

I can see he has a metal chain around his neck and both his wrists. Looking down at my own hands, I notice I don't have any. It's kind of sad knowing that I probably don't pose any sort of threat to him and so he just leaves me free. Damn, he's probably right, too.

We're probably going to rest for the day, judging by the fire Giarsh has going. He's patrolling the perimeter while we're here, hanging out. What do I do? I can't leave Erice. He's my best bet for surviving this place. I still don't know where the hell I am, but this Underlord fella doesn't sound like he's a good guy to meet.

My stomach chooses that moment to growl. What the hell, stomach? Control yourself!

"Do you dare growl at a knight, female?" Fucking hell.

I stand up to my full height to give myself some courage, despite the fact that I only stand to the top of his horse shoulder.

"Look, Giarsh. Number one, I'm not fucking growling at you. That was my stomach telling me I'm hungry. Number two, I have a damn name and it's Kinsey, not female." I'm still shaking inside, but damn, this fucker gets on my nerves with all his high and mighty. Since I stand so much taller than all of you, you guys need to bow to me shit.

"Get on your damn knees, Kinsey. That's right. That's exactly where you should always be."

I feel my face contorting from the memory that just stabbed my mind. Giarsh whinnies and it makes me fucking laugh.

Giarsh clears his throat and stomps his front feet a few times onto the ground.

"You shouldn't be hungry when there's a Rewsk right next to you. He can do without his tail." I almost choke on nothing when Erice lets out a booming laugh. What the hell is wrong with this place?

"She prefers her meat cooked. Just look at her. She's too precious for the way we eat things."

"Then cook it. What is the matter?"

"What's the matter, Kinsey? You can come and nibble on me all you want. I won't complain one bit."

Giarsh removes one of his swords and swings it down right at Erice's tail, but misses by an inch. I gulp.

Erice slowly rolls to his feet and stands up with a toothy smile. Does anything shake him?

"If you want a taste for yourself, you'll have to wait in line, knight."

Eww, no.

"Let's just find something else to eat." Giarsh's eyes flick to mine right before he sheaths his sword behind him. He picks his ax-scythe back up and continues his patrol without another word. I guess there will be no eating tonight. Erice is still staring at Giarsh's back by the time I plant my ass near the fire and lie down.

Maybe if I take a small nap, it'll take my mind off my hunger.

My body starts to warm up slowly and my eyes start that flutter that happens right before the sandman comes for you.

The belt comes down in rapid succession onto Waylon's back with a sickening whack *sound and my heart breaks for him. I'm so scared and I don't know what to do. I'm too small to stop him. The welts on his back start to rise and change in color when he finally leaves us on the floor. I crawl over to him and hold him close to me.*

Waylon's not even crying. He's just staring at the wall and rocking with me.

I wake up angry. I'm so fucking angry! The pain in my heart still echoes even when I bring myself up to a sitting position. Erice is sleeping behind me a couple of feet away, he's at the end of his chain that's attached to a nearby tree.

Giarsh is on his knees with his arms crossed and head tilted down. Is he sleeping? The thought of being taken to a damn Underlord that might torture us to death has me angry. I'm reminded of the dream. I'm reminded too much of all I don't want to feel anymore.

I don't know what compels me, but my feet are leading me softly to where Giarsh parked himself. My hands fiddle with my belt as quietly as I can, as I continue to creep up to his side. No one's breathing has changed. My heart is pounding loudly in my ears.

It feels like fucking muscle memory or something as I

start to loop a makeshift noose around his neck. I'm just about to tighten it when he grabs my arm and neck.

"I wouldn't if I were you. I could crush your neck right now and use your body to feed our hunger, but I won't. Your false bravery entertains me." These fucking guys and their entertainment. What the hell am I, a damn clown?

His hand starts to squeeze my neck slowly, and I can't help but get a little turned on. Fucking hell.

"Shh...Kinsey. They're going to hear us."

His lips devour mine as his hands start to release their restriction, making me suck in his breath. Our tongues tangle in a wet dance as he continues to thrust slowly into me to decrease the amount of noise we might make.

Giarsh's red tongue peeks out to lick his fangs, making it bleed, coating part of his teeth with crimson.

My hand lets go of the belt and Giarsh starts to let go of my neck, pushing me away from him slowly at the same time. His red eyes continue to stare into mine as his pupils start to expand and constrict every so often.

I feel fucking useless, and I'm still angry. I turn around and bring myself back to Erice's side. Fuck him too, but he's the lesser of two evils right now. Don't ask me why but when I reach him, I bury my face into his chest as close as I can just so I can get away from that damn horse.

Erice brings his arms around me and hums as we both lie down on the ground and drift off to sleep without any food at all.

CHAPTER SIX

KINSEY

I awake with a start when the body behind me is jerked away from me, almost jerking *me* backward with the momentum. It is way too early for this.

Rolling around to a sitting position, I see Giarsh and Erice in a full-blown battle of wills again. How did Erice get his weapons back? Giarsh is bucking like a wild mustang, swinging his double sword haphazardly as Erice wraps the loose chain from his wrist around Giarsh's neck. I don't know how much damage that chain is doing because Giarsh is fully covered in armor, but he's struggling to get to Erice.

Erice has a talent for somehow always getting the upper hand. I don't know how he does it, but I'm stepping back until I'm able to hide myself behind a tree trunk as I watch the show in front of me.

I let out a loud gasp when somehow Erice rips off Giarsh's helmet, revealing his true face. He looks like his skin got ripped off with the helmet, muscle strands stretching across his skull. The eye sockets are sunken in and his eyes are glowing in the darkness that contains it. His teeth and fangs are sharper than what normal human dentures should be as he starts to gnash at the air, trying to reach Erice like a beast.

Erice slips the chains in his grasp upwards towards Giarsh's neck and somehow sneaks one of his weapons right through the throat in an upward motion, the exit wound coming out from the top of Giarsh's skull.

I don't know if I'm screaming inside my head or if I'm screaming out loud as Giarsh's horse body slams into the ground unceremoniously and without any sort of grace in a loud crash that rumbles the ground beneath my feet.

Erice is quiet, breathing hard, and still has his signature smile on his face. His body is splattered in blood as he continues to rip off pieces of armor and stab whatever flesh he can see. By the time Erice is done ripping off all of Giarsh's armor, his fury has mutilated the body into something unrecognizable, something resembling hamburger meat and a horse's hindquarters.

Throwing his claws aside, Erice adopts Giarsh's double swords as his own. The swords must be made of something crazy because it's strong enough to cut through the chains that held him. Now there's a dangling chain from both his wrists and his neck, making Erice look even more menacing.

What the hell just happened? One second we were prisoners, and now?

Erice runs towards me and I start running too...away from him. He's freaking me out. Watching him take down someone like that knight solidifies my assumption that he is insane.

He jumps onto my back, trapping me beneath him. His body slides against me from all the blood that's coating him, and it makes me want to gag.

"Mmmm. You do taste particularly delicious."

His tongue travels along my neck as one of his hands brings my dress up over the curve of my ass. Fuck, I hope he doesn't eat me. Isn't that horrible? That I'd rather he rape me than eat me? What is he going to rape me with, though?

Erice grinds his crotch against my ass as his hands continue to roam across my body with no particular pattern that I can decipher.

He suddenly stands up, pulling my dress with him as he laughs out loud. What the fuck is going on? What is wrong with this guy?

Spinning me in his arms, his black tongue that's coated in Giarsh's blood starts to lick the side of my face, probably leaving a crimson smear behind. When he's done playing with me, he shoves me away and starts to walk away from the campground. What the fuck?!

What am I supposed to do? Looking at the mangle of flesh and bones near the fire pit, Giarsh's body will forever be in my nightmares. I turn quickly before I can vomit and run after Erice, because I have no other choice in this place.

When I get close enough, his tapeworm tail taps my leg, but he doesn't look back. I don't understand him, but he's all I got.

We walk for what feels like hours and finally, after entering a new cluster of trees beyond a long stretch of barren flat land, Erice decides to stop. I'm so damn tired. I don't know how I fell asleep on the ground, but when I wake up, there's already a fire going with meat roasting, and Erice is sharpening his new swords on a nearby rock.

My eyes stare at his mechanical motion, to and fro, to and fro.

"Grandma, what are you doing? You're so crazy."

"You need to keep our knives sharp, girl. How else do we filet the meat? I don't want to have to saw into it."

I watch as Grandma continues to pass the blade to and fro against the neck of the sink spout. I'm amazed at her ingenuity. I hope one day I can be as good as her with problem-solving. These are skills to keep you alive, city or no city.

"Kinsey, you grace me with your presence once more. You were lost for a minute there." Erice is handing me another skewer of meat in front of my face. Did I just blank out? I don't remember seeing him move. Wasn't he just sharpening his blade a minute ago?

"Thank you. Should I ask what this is?"

Erice smiles but doesn't say anything. I must have slept the day away because the sun is already going down by the time I finished eating the meat stick.

"Erice, I'm going to pee just right over there. I'll be back." His tail swishes a little, but he doesn't turn around. He's standing on higher ground, staring into the barren wasteland. Okay then.

Once I'm done peeing, trying to dry myself partially with some dead leaves and partially with the air, I pull my panties up and let my blood-stained dress fall back down. Why am I in a dress, anyway? I don't remember putting this on. Running my moccasins along some of the dry patches of grass nearby in case I got some pee on them, I turn to slowly walk back to our makeshift campsite.

Erice is sitting by the fire and I decide to just go back to sleep, despite the fact that I just woke up. I'll need the energy to do whatever it is we'll be doing tomorrow since this place never has a dull moment.

CHAPTER SEVEN

KINSEY

Our walk today is hot and dry. We haven't come across any rivers or lakes yet. Giarsh got rid of our water skins and now it's starting to take a toll on us. My mind is getting a little woozy the longer the orange sun beats down on me.

He can't do this!

She belongs with us! How much more can a heart take?

His arms go around me in a strong embrace, holding me, catching me before my soul crumbles. He's lending me his strength quietly, and it's the only thing that grounds me in this moment of loss.

I'm getting woozy from the flood of emotions that threaten to drown me.

I'm slowing down, I know it. Erice is getting farther and farther away, and my vision starts to blur. The ground suddenly hits my face.

The sound of metal on metal and the clinking of chains wakes me up. My mind is still groggy, like there's too much fuzz and cotton. Clarity is just within reach, but not quite yet.

Am I dreaming? *I can't move my hands, though. I want to rub my eyes to get the sand out. Why can't I move my hands? A pinch of pain and my eyes fly open. It's still so fuzzy the way abrupt awakenings are.*

It's too damn bright, but I need to see. I need to see what's happening. My arm feels warm from the inside. The warmth traveling upwards.

Blinking a few times to clear my vision, I see a firepit in front of me; the warmth emanating every time the flames lick upwards. The sound of hooves come closer and closer, making the ground vibrate. I must be going out of my damn mind, because the sight of Giarsh's mutilated flesh is still ingrained into my mind like a brand.

But there he is, in all his knightly glory. Giarsh. How can this be? He's dead. I saw it!

"You've awakened." That's not Giarsh's voice. That's *not* his voice.

"Who are you?" My voice sounds a bit dry, with a crackle at the end. I'm so thirsty.

The knight comes towards me and bends his forelegs down. His human torso bends down enough to help assist my body up into a sitting position. I didn't notice it until his hand reaches for it, but he's bringing what looks like a waterskin towards my lips. Both of my hands automatically shoot up to steady it and to drink the water with as much greed as I possibly can. I almost drown myself when I notice that the sound of chains is coming from my wrists. *I'm chained by the wrist*. When he takes the water skin away from me, dripping cool water all over my chin and chest, I pick my hands up and notice that they're chained together with about a foot of leeway in between them.

"Where's Erice?"

"I found you alone. There were no others." Did he abandon me? I remember hitting the ground. That fucker left me behind.

"Why are my hands chained up? I didn't do anything wrong. What could I have done when I was passed out?" His red eyes flicker, but his expression doesn't change.

"You are to be taken to the Underlord's Keep. It was best to prevent any trouble from happening. We are about a day's walk from our destination." I don't like the sound of that. I don't like the sound of this damn Underlord. What does he want with me, anyway? How does he even know I'm here? I don't want to go where he wants us to go. I need to think of something.

"I'm hungry. I require my food to be cooked. Please." If Giarsh was here, he'd be telling me to chew on Erice. But Erice isn't here either. I hope this distraction works. Maybe Erice is looking for me? It sucks to not know if I can depend on that bastard.

Instead of a giant ax to wield, he has a giant serrated spear, one that he now stabs into the hard sunbaked ground. I watch as he loops another chain around it, the chain that's attached to the ones around my wrist. I guess he doesn't want me to run away. I wish I could, but I am still pretty exhausted and I really am hungry now that I mentioned it.

So yes, I'm willing to sit here while he goes hunting or whatnot.

I watch as the horse guy goes to leave. I never did get his damn name.

I have my back up against a tree and my head is starting to loll a bit.

"Psst."

I try to blink my eyes a few times, but my head still feels so damn heavy.

"Psst. Pssssstttt."

What the fuck? Is that a snake or something? The thought makes me open my eyes wide and I start looking around my ass that's currently sitting on the ground. Fuck, I hope it's not a snake.

A rock hits my damn shoulder and now I'm shivering from fear because there better not be a snake above my head!

The craziest thing happens though. Behind a tree that's a few yards ahead of me pops out. Not one, but two heads on either side of the trunk. I think they're both girls, they look feminine. Their hair is tied in strange bun-like pigtails on each side of their head. Are they identical twins or something?

"Psst."

"Hey."

So, it was them, not a snake, who was calling to me. Their skin has a strange pallor, very corpse-like. Their eyes are covered in the deep purple ribbon that also covers their pigtails. The girl with ribbons covering both her eyes flicks her finger to me in a come hither motion, showing me her long nails.

They're nuts, can't they see I'm bound? I shake my wrist

in front of me a little and the second girl, who has one eye exposed since the ribbon only covers her nose and other eye, moves her sight to my wrists.

They both disappear behind the tree trunk again, but I can hear them whispering to each other. When they jump out fully from behind the trunk, I almost cuss out loud. What the everloving hell is happening here?

They're Siamese twins, joined at the hip. They have two separate torsos but share the hips and legs. Wait, the more I look, the more I see that they're both missing an arm. Each sister is missing an opposite arm towards the center. Their breasts are covered in the same purple ribbon edged with gold, attached to a large gold necklace. The skirt is the most bizarre thing because it's draped and beautiful like theater drapes, but there are small skulls that adorn the bottom hem of their skirt. It kind of looks like bird skulls, but knowing how crazy this place is, it could be something else entirely.

"What's this then?"

"Have you found trouble?

"Do you need escape?"

"We can assist."

"If you will have our help, that is."

"The cost is cheap, you see."

"It will be quick."

"So easy."

Holy shit, they speak like they're sharing one mind. It's creepy as hell.

"Yeah, I need to get free before that knight comes back."

"You agree then?"

"Pay to play."

"She will."

"She looks like a player."

The twins skip over and do a little twirl before they take out a damn glowing staff from who knows where. There's a skull at the top with a spinal cord still attached that winds around the shaft of the staff. I'm staring at the skull, trying to decide if it's human when green flames burst forth and the twin holding it starts to spin it like she's in a damn parade. It doesn't even emit the sound of a live flame roaring, it's just silent. It doesn't emit a smell either. Next, she tosses it mid-spin and the other twin grabs it with a curtsey and waves the flame across my chains. My eyes widen in wonder as my wrist chains drop to the ground. By the time I look up, the staff has disappeared again and the girls are smiling at me. It would be sweet if it weren't for the yellow-stained piranha teeth poking through their gums. Fucking hell, this place is like hell.

I swear I hear the stomping of hooves in the distance, making me jump to my feet. We need to go now. Before I can ask the girls where they're headed, they grab me and throw me onto their...backs? They run like a gazelle while I'm trying to hold on to both of their shoulders, riding piggyback. Did I say gazelle? Because the longer we run, the girls fall to all fours and run just like a damn beast while maintaining their form.

The wind is whipping my face so hard, deafening my ears, that I have to keep my head down between their shoulders. When the running starts to slow down, I can feel the ache in my *own* shoulders from trying to hold on to them in such a wide position.

We find another cluster of trees by a cliff and stop. They drop me unceremoniously onto the damp ground as they start jumping up and down, shaking their arms like they're readying for a fight or something.

With a small twirl, they turn to face me, and their piranha smiles are back on their faces.

"You pay to play."

"Play to pay."

"The game begins."

"Choose your player."

"There's only one board."

"Dive on in."

"What game? How do I choose a player if I don't even know what we're playing? Is this the price? I don't even know what price I agreed to?"

I'm laying partially on my back, propped on my elbows, trying to figure out this crazy talk coming out of them. They start walking slowly towards me and I'm getting a little freaked out. *What price? Is it my life?*

I'm like a deer in headlights as they get on hands and knees to crawl towards me like a spider. What the hell is going on right now? One of their hands shoots and grabs me by the ankle with a firm grip, their long nails grazing my skin, and I don't know if I should scream or run because who the hell am I running to?

The other twin starts to lick her purple tongue up my kneecaps and it makes me shiver in disgust, the wet spot on my knee cooling when a breeze comes by. Was this the price? Fuck, I'm stuck between a rock and a hard place because they did free me after all. Damnit!

I lay back down and cover my eyes with my arms because I'm just going to have to go through with this. I have to pay to play. The game already started, and I didn't even know I was part of it.

I can't look, because if I do then I might chicken out. Maybe they'll just do me and leave me. I'm fine with that. They're not going to eat me, right? Fuck, I'm really doing this. These girls are freaky. It's just sex, right?

One of their hands lifts my dress and another rips my panties, making me gasp in shock from the sting of the elastic breaking. I do remove my arm from my face then to make sure I'm seeing what I'm seeing. One of the girl's piranha teeth is nipping at my inner thigh, while the other girl's hand is grabbing one of my breasts. She's grabbing really hard too because I whimper and want to cry. It hurts!

When one of the girls opens her mouth wide, like she's about to take a bite out of my pussy for dinner, I scream and try to kick them away. *Fuck yes, I'm chicken, I changed my mind!* The other twin is laughing as she pushes my legs further apart with a strength I can't combat from my submissive position on the ground.

One of the girls starts to lick my mound, and I close my eyes to brace myself for the bite. There's a rattle of chains and suddenly the twins are pulled off me, leaving welts and streaks of blood behind on my thigh and ribs from their claws.

Ignoring the pain, I push myself up to sitting to see what the fuck happened. *Dear lord.*

It's Erice, he's wrapped the chain a few more times around both their necks preventing them from taking a bite out of him. Their arms are flailing and scratching at his muscles, but he doesn't seem to care one bit. He's thrusting on top of them, and I can't pull my eyes away. *What the actual fuck?*

The girls have something bloody and phallic-looking between their legs. Erice's thrusting is enveloping it in his ... folds, making it tinge pink and glisten in the sun, the sounds of squelching getting louder and louder. He thrusts a few more times and when they're buried to the hilt; the twins scream in pure agony. Erice laughs his booming laugh and pulls himself away. Blood is trailing down his crotch. When I look at the girls, I see that whatever Erice has between his legs has totally ripped or bitten off the twins' phallus. The metallic smell of it mixed with sex fills the air, only adding to the chill going down my spine.

My mind is going a million miles a minute because I'm trying to understand how twin girls have a damn phallus and how a male like Erice has a crotch opening that eats phalluses. Erice stands up and starts to rub the blood and slime from his crotch all over his abs and chest while he watches the girls writhe in pain beneath him. Is this fucking turning him on? He's crazy!

I see a shiver run down his spine right before he lunges at the twins and starts cannibalizing their necks. The sound of crunching makes me turn away. I'm trying to hold in my gag. Should I have stayed with the knight instead? Fucking Erice is a monster too. Everyone in this damn place is a monster.

I'm fighting, but all their hands are holding me down. What was supposed to be friendly faces warp into something terrifying. There's that damn pinch again and sure enough, the fight leaves me even though my mind screams until the blackness takes over.

My heart is beating erratically, and my breaths are haggard. I think I'm going to make a run for it while Erice is still devouring the twins. Slowly but surely, I make it past a few trees, my feet slipping every so often, before a hard and warm body tackles me to the ground. My bones can't take all this rattling. The twigs and pebbles underneath me have given me road rash. At least my head didn't take too much of a brunt in the fall. Looking forward, I can see his arms in front of me, covered in inky blackish-red blood. The smell is still as copper as any other type of blood.

He nuzzles me and the creepiest part is how sweet his voice sounds against the back of my neck, his warm breath moving my hair. "Hello precious."

CHAPTER EIGHT

KINSEY

I guess I'm back with Erice. Where this fucker was when I was captured, I have no clue and it also looks like he doesn't really give a rat's ass either.

We did at least find a camp spot closer to a river of sorts. Erice left me by the campfire to wash up while he went out to find food, I guess. He didn't tell me a thing before he left.

Washing blood out of a light dress is a disaster. All it does is leave a pink tinge behind, but it will have to do. My body is just about dried from my quick dip in the cold river when I hear footsteps coming up behind me making me squeak and hold my damp dress in front of me.

"Relax, little bit. It's just me. Here, take this and fill it up with some water. You're still looking a little rough around the edges there." I can't wrap my head around the guy that just devoured a sentient creature in front of me and this guy who's worried because I'm looking a little rough for wear.

I am thirsty though. Quickly putting my damp dress

back on, I grab the waterskin he hands me and I almost drop it. It's the same ribbon from the twins' face, hair, and skirt. I don't know how I feel about this. How are waterskins made? My fucking god, they're made of stomachs aren't they? Did he just...turn the twins into water skins and adorn it with ribbon? I want to gag but at the same time, we fucking need water skins for our trek. Look at what happened the last time I became dehydrated. I want to hate him, be disgusted by him but I can't because of his damn ingenuity.

"Precious, we don't have all day now." I snatch the waterskin from his hand and do as I'm told. I can hear him laughing behind me as the flames from the campfire grow.

Once the skins are full, I toss it to his chest and sit by the campfire. Is it petty? Probably. I hate that he's always laughing at something, and I don't know if that something is him thinking of how he's going to cook me up next.

The food tastes different from the last creature I ate. This one is, for some reason, spicier. I don't know how that makes me feel. Am I going to be able to digest it? Is it going to be fire coming out of my ass? Do I even want to know where this meat came from?

Lying down on my side, I stare into the campfire and just absorb the warmth. My dress is dry now, so it's not as uncomfortable. Erice lies down behind me like he always does and wraps his arm around my waist. I don't know how I feel about this, and I don't think it matters. Would I really make it out there without him? Probably not. I need him.

"Kinsey, I got you some flamin' hot Cheetos."

"You did! How? He's going to kill you if he found you stole his money!"

"It's not like that, Kinsey. I found some coins here and there. It's just a small bag of Cheetos."

"Thank you so much! I'll share it, okay. We'll eat it slowly, together." I give him the tightest hug I possibly can. He's so sweet to me, this is why I love him so much. The bag of Cheetos is dropped on the ground as he returns my hug.

Our embrace lasts longer than it should. His hands start to roam my back, sneaking under my top, and it sparks something inside my gut. I feel butterflies in my stomach. It feels empty and aching all at once. How does he do this to me? How does he always make me feel this way? Like it's the first time all over again. We shouldn't. *Why does something so wrong feel so right, though?*

My breasts started coming out when I hit the age of sixteen, a couple of years ago. He's seven years older than me, and that simple fact just makes me even hotter. It's so naughty, it isn't right. But it just makes me want it more. We're each other's firsts and that fact makes my heart swell. I don't regret losing my virginity at sixteen one bit.

We're already both sitting down since the hug, so it was easy for him to push me onto my back. That and I offer no resistance when he pushes me, though I know I should. A good girl would, right? The floor beneath me is cold and hard, but it does nothing to cool down the embers heating up inside of me. The anticipation of what's to come has my heart beating faster. I want it so badly.

He presses his soft lips onto mine and after a few more sweet presses, his tongue starts to peek out for an invitation. Despite opening up for him, his tongue still traces the seam of my lips slowly and languidly, making me press my thighs together. How does he turn me on so fast? Have I just become wanton? Does that make me a dirty girl? But I don't want anyone else.

Our lips and tongues start a sensuous dance as his hands

roam the side of my body, only giving my breasts the barest of touches. The tease is tantalizing, and I can feel myself pressing back up against him in an effort to just feel more of him. I need more.

When my face starts to feel flush from our tongues dueling, he finally presses his body fully down on top of mine, forcing my squirming into submission.

My legs fall open, welcoming his heat, welcoming the hardness between his legs. The skirt I have on does nothing to hide what he has going on down there. It's hot, it's hard as a pipe, and it's rubbing my panties against my wet folds, bumping my clit along the way. The friction is glorious and torturous.

He takes his lips off mine to rip off my top and comes right back for round two of kissing. My lips feel abused, but I love it. I'm only in a bralette and his hands are molding to my breast, wanting to replace my cups. His hands are so large and warm. When his tongue starts to trace my jawline, I shiver from the coolness it leaves behind.

The stubble on his face scrapes my shoulder as he continues to plant kisses down my body. His fingers scratch my skin a little when he rips the bralette down, making my breast pop out. When his warm mouth engulfs my nipple and sucks, my back arches a bit, and I let out a low moan. How can I not? My god, his mouth. Sometimes it's hard to keep the noise down when it feels so damn good, but we can't get caught. That fact makes it all the hotter. It makes him nip and bite me even more to see how much I can control myself.

I love the fact that he gives both of my breasts equal attention. The other nipple starts to pucker as the wetness cools my skin from abandonment. His hands are playing with my pussy, all the while his mouth plays with my breasts. So much sensation at once. It took us more than a few tries before I was able to reach my first orgasm. Ever since, he's been chasing it to see how fast he can make me cum before he sticks his dick in me. But he must be impatient today, because now I can hear the faint sound of his zipper and pants being shoved down.

He comes back up to kiss my mouth as he grinds his cock against me, behind his boxers. Seems I'm not the only one who is having a hard time keeping it quiet as he moans into my mouth, forcing me to swallow it down for him.

We both grind against each other until it feels like my panties are going to give me rug burn down there. I can't take it; I want him so badly. It's my *little hands that start ripping his boxers off as he chuckles into our kiss that hasn't stopped. Our breaths are hot and heavy as I start to stroke his hard dick in my hand. I can feel the precum leaking at the tip and I use my finger to swirl it all over his head, making him groan again.*

We're so in sync that we both pull back just enough so he can shove his cock into me, so he can bring it home where it belongs. No matter how many times we do this, he still feels too damn big for me. The stretch of my lower lips, the feel of his cock filling me up to the brim. He doesn't care one bit as he shoves himself in even harder so his pelvic bones hit my own. The hair over his cock starts to tease my clit the more he grinds me into the damn floor, like he can't get close enough.

I'm already so wet but I want more. I need more. My hands roam down his back and grab his ass to bring him closer into me. Our height difference makes him breathe over my shoulder as my teeth bite down on his to stifle my cries of ecstasy.

He lifts one of my legs over his shoulder and starts pounding, making my already sensitive insides start to chase something that feels too far to reach. Too soon, he brings himself behind me without detaching us and crosses his arms over my chest and waist. The embrace makes me want to cry with how sweet it is.

His thrusts have slowed down, making me savor the slide of his cock in and out of me as I feel him peppering kisses along the crook of the back of my neck. The hand on my waist travels down and down until it reaches my clit and starts to circle and tug, teasing me to a higher plane of pleasure and sensations despite his slow pace. He plays my body like it's his own and that fact makes me push against his thrust to hurry the chase. I need this. It feels so good, but just not there yet. Almost ... almost...

"I love the way your pussy feels when it starts to squeeze me. Do you want my cum inside you, Kinsey?" He does this. These sweet whispers against the shell of my ear, just quiet enough for it to be for my ears only. The intimacy has my pussy squeezing again.

"Please, please cum in me. I need to feel you. Give it all to me." I'm on the pill. I was able to sneak out to the clinic to get some, just for these moments.

He pinches my clit and starts to ram into me harder from behind when the tell-tale signs of my fall come closer. He can probably feel it too because his free hand moves from my chest to cover my mouth as I moan out loud from my climax. He milks the sensation for only a few moments and then pushes me against the floor and starts ramming into me to chase his own release. The scrapes I might get on my cheeks are worth it...so worth it...

I'm lost in the memory, and I can feel my hips gyrating. Fuck, am I touching myself? Am I awake? Was I dreaming? *Those aren't my fingers.*

Erice glides his claws along my wet folds and I can't help but respond. I must have been having a wet dream and he's doing things to me. It feels too damn good to care where his claws have been. One of his arms is holding me across the chest and the familiar position makes me want to cry. It almost feels the same. Like I'm back. I need him so bad. Erice is just going to have to do, whatever it is his fingers are doing.

The moan that escapes my lips dies quickly when my body is suddenly thrown onto its back with unnecessary force. Erice runs both of his claws down my front sending shivers and goosebumps across my skin as his face goes lower... and lower...

Oh my god... is he...

That large black tongue of his dives into my pussy without any sort of preamble and starts to probe, probe deep. The groan he lets out sends vibrations across my lower lips and clit making my hips thrust forward into his face. He takes it as an invitation because both of his hands grab my ass and push my pussy harder into his face.

That tongue...that black tongue is doing wicked, wicked things to me. It shouldn't feel this good. It feels like a fucking dick that has a mind of its own, with the ability to do way too many things I can't even begin to describe. When his teeth nip my clit, and his tongue dives back in, my legs clap around his head and I throw my own back to let out a cry of pleasure. Shit, I can feel my pussy pulsating as he continues to hammer into me with just his tongue. The stretch he's giving me is making it feel even better.

The waves that come with the aftermath of this climax are almost as bad as the peak itself. His tongue is lapping up everything I have to offer and even starts licking the inside of my thigh. He's so fucking nasty, but I can't help but get turned on by that fact.

When his lips close over my clit and start to suck to almost the point of pain, I swear I feel another climax building. But being the bastard he is, he stops his sucking right before it hits and just gives me another long swipe with the flat of his tongue before he climbs up over me with a toothy smile full of fangs.

Fucking tease.

I'm so mad.

I'm so frustrated.

When it looks like he wants to swipe that black tongue of his inside my mouth, I turn my head aside and push against his shoulders. He laughs and rolls off me in that cocky way he always does, putting both hands behind his head once he's relaxed onto his back. He acts like nothing even happened.

His crotch region is full of slime, and I'm reminded of where I am. This fucking hell with this fucking bastard who left me for dead and devoured a creature right before my damn eyes like it was nothing. I can't stand his fucking company, but I have no other choice. Ugh!

I roll back over to my side and close my eyes to try and go back to sleep.

CHAPTER NINE

KINSEY

We're walking along the barren plains instead of between tree clusters today. The moccasins Erice fashioned for me are starting to wear thin on the bottom. I tried to wash and dry them when we camped by the river, but the bloodstains are still all over it, like I never even tried.

Erice still walks around butt naked with his cross strap and double sword he swiped off of Giarsh's dead body. I should be disturbed by this, but if it helps to keep us alive, I'll take it.

The sky seems more orange today. Is it just me? Or has my vision just become so accustomed to the overcast of orange over everything?

"Erice, where am I? I need to get home. I don't even know how I got here."

"You entertain me. Stop your nonsense, little bit. If you're here, it means you've always been here. There's no other way. The more you ramble, the more I start to worry about your mental stability."

Fucker says I'm the one that's crazy. He's fucking crazy! His existence...and everyone's existence here is fucking crazy. I'm not going to ask him about it anymore. I hate his stupid answers.

Horse hooves start getting louder and by now, I know what it means. I start running towards Erice. I don't have to look back to know who's coming.

Erice looks back, though, and fucking smiles. I hate him.

I start to hate him even more when he cuts one of my calves with his sword and jumps over my fallen body like he's doing the fucking hurdles. When I pick my head up after having face planted into the ground and spitting out the dust from my mouth, I see he's fucking skipping away. He skips and leaps like a kangaroo onto a nearby boulder and then onto a dead tree, climbing it like a spider monkey.

Me? I'm here again, left behind. Fucker!

The hooves come to an abrupt halt in front of me, kicking up even more dust into my face. I shield what I can with my arm, but this place is a fucking dustbowl. I'm manhandled up...and up and suddenly I'm face to face with the second horse guy I've come across. He's holding me under my armpits like I'm a damn toddler. You know what, with how enormous he is, that's what I look like next to him.

"You seem well. I shall return you on our path since you are no longer lost." I hiss a little as my leg flexes and my calf wound bites into me.

"You are wounded. You will not be able to make the trek

we must cover." With that statement, he tosses me onto his damn back like a ... horse rider.

He has spiked armor back here too but there's a small smooth part right where his horse back dips. Maybe he was made to be ridden? Why does that sound so nasty? Why am I even considering a damn...dark demonic centaur knight that way?

I hold on as best as I can, but his armor is pretty slick to the touch. You would think my clammy hands would help with the friction. But no. He doesn't trot, but gallops at full speed ahead. What is the damn hurry? My long black hair whips behind me, and I cringe at the thought of the tangles that are forming. I know it's trivial, but I love my hair.

He slows to a trot after what feels like a couple of hours, and I take the opportunity to look around us. *Woah.*

Everything looks like actual hell around here. Barren plains, the ground cracking like we're in a desert. Smoke billows from all the cracks and there's...there's...skeletons of all sorts scattered around. In fact, I can hear the crunch of this horse guy's hooves going over it, making me cringe. I can't tell what part belongs to what and there are spears jutting out from the ground with randomly shaped skulls perched on top of it. *Eesh.* If this isn't a 'fuck off' message, I don't know what is.

As we start to crest the small uphill climb, sharp black spikes start to appear in the distance. The spikes keep growing and growing the more steps we take, connecting to something enormous. Holy mackerel, is that the 'keep'. It's more of a castle of fucking doom, pitch black and ominous, sucking the life out of the air that surrounds it.

The sight of it must give horse guy a second wind

because he starts speed racing again. The more the castle is revealed to me, the more I feel a sense of dread.

My eyes widen even more at the sight in front of me. Not only is it a castle on a damn hill... said hill has the shape of a fucking skull carved into it. A skull with his maws open. There is a waterfall that exits its mouth like it's spitting its 'fuck you' to the world beneath it.

"Hey. Hey!" I'm tapping the side of his body to get his attention.

Horse guy slows to a gallop as he turns his torso to look at me. I guess he doesn't need to look at where he's going. He probably knows this place like the back of his hand.

"What's your name?"

He smiles a sinister smile and the way his eyes roam my body; I feel a chill. Shit. Don't. Please don't.

"I am Isra." Oh, why does he sound so flirtatious, or maybe he's sizing me up to see if I taste good? This place. When did this become my norm? I shouldn't even like this guy; he's trying to take me somewhere I don't need to be!

"I'm Kinsey." I'll give him that, but that's it.

He gives me a toothy grin right before he starts sprinting again towards the castle of doom.

I'm trying to hold on for dear life and not slide off his back when my heart falls into the pit of my stomach. There's a cliff up ahead. What the fuck? He's not slowing down either. Shit, shit, shit.

Before I can even decide on a course of action to make Isra stop what he's doing, he leaps into the air. My scream is left behind in the wind as I hold on to his torso with my nails digging into his armor. We're going to fall to our deaths. What is wrong with him?

Instead of dying, we land on another cliff edge that runs along the lower levels, my chest slamming into his back. The wind gets knocked out of my lungs on the landing, but I'm too in shock to bite Isra's head off. He just continues to gallop like he's done it a million times, and he probably has. This cliff edge still makes me feel like we're going to fall to our doom any second, but the farther he gallops, the wider the edge becomes.

It starts to climb uphill, opening up to a wider path that can probably accommodate two cars side by side. Is this some sort of backway into the castle? No, because we're still coming up to the front entrance, it seems.

A gasp escapes my lips as Isra slows to a trot again. All along this road are nightmares to be seen. Nightmares on top of nightmares. Is this part of the damn decor? There are prisoners chained all along the ground in no particular pattern. Peeking to the right, I see a male creature of some sort. His head is encased in a round metal contraption that looks like it's seen better days. The metal is fully rusted out, giving it a reddish hue. There are spikes jutting out in some areas and small holes in others. At least he can breathe through it, I guess. His back has a damn missile or bomb strapped to him. The weight of it weighing him down to the point where he has to trudge along like he has a hunchback. His hands, lord his hands. Both arms are trapped in a free floating pillory like the ones from the medieval times. His wrists are scratched and wounded from having it on for who knows how long. The pillory stained in old blood.

The crazy thing? No one is moaning in pain. It's like a ghost town of tortured prisoners aimlessly walking like zombies.

All the other guys we pass by are some sort of variation of this. Instead of their head being fully encapsulated with a metal ball, some have metal collars so tall that it covers half their face. The face that is exposed has skin ripped off and I can see part of their skull. They can't walk far because all of them have chains on their ankles with only so much leeway to allow them to move around.

No. One. Makes. A. Sound. That's the creepiest part about it all.

Another strange thing about this... garden of the walking dead is that they're all males. Why?

Isra trots past the 'garden' and the size of the castle casts a darkness and gloom over the ground. This place is huge and very foreboding. You can feel the menace radiating off it. Or perhaps that's just my mind playing tricks on me. Maybe this black castle of doom is actually all flowers and rainbows inside. Who knows?

I highly doubt it.

The doorway is massive, well beyond eight feet tall. It opens like a mouth with jagged edges on top that reminds me of teeth. If this is what the opening looks like, what will the bowels have in store for us? Will I be chewed up and spit out, to be planted in the garden with the others? I shouldn't even agree to this!

I attempt to slide off Isra's back mid trot, uncaring if I take injuries in the fall, but his reflexes are too quick. His human arms hold on tight and I don't know what comes over me, but I start kicking him. I'm thrashing like a crazy person because I do not want to know what's in that stupid castle. I don't know how I do it, but I slip from his grasp and hit the concrete ground with a thud. It hurts like crazy, but I tamp down the pain and scrabble to get away beneath his hooves. Being this low, his human torso can't grab onto me, and judging from our horseback ride here, I don't think he wants to trample me to death, or else he would have already.

I'm already beyond the doorway and this place is dark. The orange glow from the outside isn't helping much at all, there are too many twists and turns, corners and creepy decor on the walls. But all these obstacles also help me hide myself better.

I slip on something wet on the ground and when I jut my hand out to stabilize myself, the wall is coated with something more than dust. What the hell? Bringing my hand to my face, I try to decipher what I just touched and I swear it's the same stuff that comes off a moth's wing. On the wall, though? That doesn't make any sense...

Horse hooves are clopping slowly around the area, the sound echoing against the walls. He's looking for me. Thank goodness for these moccasins and my dark hair. My footsteps are quiet as I creep along the shadows. The dust is getting coated under my fingers as I continue to feel along the wall to help me not run into things. Something brushes against my finger rather than my finger brushing against it and I want to let out a squeal, but I hold it in and swallow down the sound.

Whatever it is jumps next to me and starts skittering across the floor like a damn crab. What the hell? The dust the creature kicks up in its quick escape goes up my nose and I try to breathe in and out of my mouth while rubbing under my nose with my wrist to stop the sneeze from coming. My body forces me to take a short intake of air, the first stages of a sneeze, and I have to consciously make an effort to close off my mouth and shut my eyes to stop it from happening. The sneeze happens quietly inside my mouth, making it ache, but I open my eyes the moment I can and start looking around. Shit, I hope Isra didn't catch that.

Something tries to grab my elbow and I do scream then.

"I'm required to take you to the Underlord. Come, let's stop this nonsense."

His spiked armor is getting caught between a couple of pillars. One of the moments I am so glad he's such a large guy because he won't be able to squeeze in any closer. I'm struggling a little bit, but after putting one of my legs up on the closest pillar and pushing, I was able to slip out of his grasp again and run the opposite direction.

What the hell does this Underlord want with me anyway? How does he even know who I am and that I'm here? It's some creepy shit when you think about it.

I've been dodging fallen pillars, broken statues, and ugly ass looking gargoyles. Why are they on the inside of this keep and not the outside? When one of the gargoyles morph and tries to grab my leg, I yelp and leap over his swipe. Fucking hell, this place! When I glance back to see if he's chasing me, all I see is a statue sitting there with his ugly mug. I'm going nuts. The hallway starts to open up and an orange glow is spilling in from the outside, allowing me to see my path a bit better.

This is both good and bad because it means Isra will see me better and have more room to make a grab. The farther I run down, my eyes catch something along the walls with dusty dark Victorian peeling wallpaper. It looks like there's a trap door in the wall, I can just see the seam separating. Do I take the chance? Might be some crazy shit in there. There's crazy shit out here too. Fuck it.

The door luckily opens up without a sound. I try to close it back slowly in case the creak wants to show up later. It's dark and musty in here but I'm slowly putting one foot in front of the other. There's a glow up ahead and it's dancing. There must be some sort of light by fire. My feet quicken as the tunnel's glow becomes brighter and brighter. There's a sconce on the wall. Despite the disgusting spider webs wrapped around the handle, I lift it off its hold. Feeling a little braver now that I have the power of light and flame with me, I start to more confidently walk down the dark and winding tunnel. How long is this thing?

The tunnel suddenly starts to take on a cobbled pathway. What the? A few more yards and it just breaks off. The hallway ends and now I'm standing at the mouth of what looks like a giant cavern. The musty smell is gone but in its place is a moldy smell. There's a hole of sorts at the very top, shining down an orange glow in a single beam aimed right at the middle of the cavern. The surrounding areas are still shrouded by some form of darkness and shadows. Where do I go from here? Is there a way out or is this a dead end? Should I turn back around?

The rattling of chains makes me snap my head to the right. There's a figure walking and dragging something. The gait is off like they can't control their limbs right. The back is rounded but it sometimes can straighten it every now and again. The sound of metal dragging across the stone and concrete grates against my ears. When the creature takes a turn and starts to walk toward the middle of the cavern, what lights up makes me take a step back. I have to blink a few times to make sure I'm seeing what I'm seeing. What the hell?

It's an emaciated female with the skin, the pallor of death or a human corpse, but I'm not sure if she's human. Her breasts are sagging and look deflated, being drug down by the metal gauges through her nipples. Her torso is strapped in heavy metal that is attached to a belt made from rusted metal medallions. The skirt and only thing that provides her with any sort of modesty is torn to shreds and faded, only covering her front and back with a long rectangular strip. Chains adorn her thighs, wrapping it in an embrace until it reaches her lower legs encased in a metal spiked cage. It reminds me of the external fixators that patients have when they break their bones. A cage to stabilize the bone, but she's walking just fine. Her upper arms are adorned with spiked braces until it reaches her lower arms that are encased by the same metal spiked cages. I can't see her head because it is also encased by a ... cube. A fucking metal cube. No wonder she can't lift her head up all the way. Each side of the cube has a face like it's mocking the wearer. Some faces are laughing, some are screaming, all with blood-red eyes. Each corner of the cube is adorned with spikes the length of my hand.

Her back has spikes that are mixed in with long, pitch-black feathers. Her cape, if you can call it that, is a cape of chains that lead to hooks at the end. The hooks remind me of teeth, waiting for unsuspecting prey to stumble upon its trap. What is she fishing for?

I'm stuck where I'm standing. It's a vision out of my nightmares. What is she? Who is she? Why does she wander? The sound of the chains' rattle matches the cadence of her walk. It's rhythmic, and it's eerie. Like a sound that warns you of your end to come. Another rattling of chains responds to hers from the other side of the cavern. She lifts her head and I swear the face on the cube morphs into a snarl. Its blood-red eyes focused on the origin of the sound. She picks up her pace, and it almost looks like she jogs towards whoever dares to move in her presence.

The other creature comes into view and out of the darkness of where it was lurking. Lord have mercy. It's ... something. Two arms, two legs, a head, but the arms look like multiple arms continuing to grow out of it until the last clawed arm reaches its ankles. The head, it's missing a face because it's been torn asunder from the top of his forehead all the way down to his crotch. How it's still alive, I have no clue. The ribs are torn apart, and it looks like it has a second spinal cord down the front of him. The legs look like the skin is in tatters, almost as if it was cloth and not skin at all, but the dark, dirty grey shade would make you think otherwise.

It stumbles and walks towards the female creature as she now starts to sprint towards him. How she jumps that high with all the metal she wears. I will never know. She leaps into the air like a panther and takes the new creature down to the ground, shredding his already torn skin even more. She's almost a blur, like a wolverine. The sound of chains jingling, and creature growls fills the cavern in echoes, making you feel like you're the one being surrounded and mauled. My eyes dart about the room like I'm trying to visually see the sounds bouncing on the walls. When they land back on the fight, all that's left of the new guy is tatters and mangled flesh in random locations. You would never even know what he looked like originally or that he was even bipedal.

The female just gets up slowly and starts her slow trudging in the cavern again, like nothing ever happened. I'm horrified, more so by her nonchalance than what she just did to that creature. What is this place? Is this where things go to die? Is she the garbage disposal of this keep? I'm now afraid to make a sound in case her attention is cast on me, but what do I do? How can I proceed without her hearing me? I can't go back the way I came...can I? I'm starting to consider just that when another sound enters the cavern.

The corners of this place must be really dark, because I didn't even know there was a ledge of sorts on the opposite end. Something big gets shoved into the cavern off this ledge and lands with a loud thud that reverberates. The female creature's head straightens up and I must be seeing things because the cube on her head starts to click click click as it turns like a damn wind-up doll. Only every time it turns, the faces on the cube start to morph into different features. How the hell...?

The solid mass on the ground starts to stir with a low, masculine moan. The female creature's head stops its slow spin and lands on a face that looks horrendous. I can't even describe it, but I wouldn't want it pointed at me. The down-turned mouth is actually starting to leak something akin to blood, but the color is off somehow. The liquid drips onto the female's chest, coating her skin right between her sagging breasts. The clinking and jingling of chains start to sound louder as she trudges toward his direction to most likely 'take out the trash'.

I see the thing on the ground shaking his head and the

arms trying to push itself up. In a flurry, the thing gets onto his feet....hooves. *Oh dear.*

The sound of hooves clopping starts to mingle with the sounds of the chains, as the female starts to pick up her pace. She really loves her job, doesn't she? The centaur lets out a masculine roar as he turns around and brings his hind legs up and kicks her right in the center, tossing her across the cavern with a loud crash. The way the darkness envelopes her, it looks like she got devoured by blackness.

When the centaur turns around, he lets out a growl and starts to walk towards the middle, towards the beam of light. Exposed muscle strands stretching across his skull with sunken eye sockets that house eyes that are blood red. His teeth and fangs are sharper than what normal human dentures should be, the exposed gums giving him a nightmarish appeal. His face is different from Giarsh though because there is a long gash and scar that cuts across his right eye socket down to the tail end of his mouth, the skin looking charred. When he opens his mouth to speak, my blood runs cold.

"Try again, Grapner. A knight of the Underlord doesn't surrender that easily." Good lord, it's Isra. What the hell? How did he end up tossed in here? Isn't this where creatures go to die?

The female starts ticking again with that head thing she does, *click click click click*, and trudges back into the light. It's like a face off and Isra looks all for it. What is wrong with him? When the female starts to sprint and jingle, Isra brings up his forelegs in anticipation. The collision that happens makes me grind my teeth with how vicious it is. Blood is being sprayed from both parties; the scars more prominent on Isra's horse part. He manages to turn again and gives her a good kick that sends her flying back once more. The sound of her hitting the far end of the cavern walls makes a sick, squelching crunch sound.

A gasp leaves my mouth right at that exact moment, and Isra's blood-red eyes snap to where I'm standing. Shit. I also forgot that I'm still holding the sconce, which means he definitely knows it's me. I turn to run for it but the sound of horse hooves beating the rocky ground gets louder and louder until I'm swept off my feet and the sconce lands on the floor; the flame getting snuffed out on its landing allowing the darkness to envelop us.

CHAPTER TEN

ISRA

I thought the little female would have found her way out of the keep by now, but it seems I have overestimated her. It must have been the Rewsk who has kept her alive this long. The Rewsk who abandoned her to her death. What is their relationship? The sound of the Grapner's ticking floats to my ears and I know time is running out. The she-demon doesn't stop until her mission is complete and her mission is to annihilate anything in her path. I need to remove us before she accomplishes what she's set out to do.

My hooves carry me quickly towards Kinsey, and my arms swoop her up before she has the chance to run any deeper into the tunnel. She must have fainted from the abrupt jerking movement of the catch because she doesn't respond anymore after my embrace. The ticking sound is getting closer, and I turn my torso around just quick enough to bring my hind legs up for another kick. One thing about killing machines like this one, it doesn't have a mind of its own besides its one task. The sound of the thud from the Grapner hitting the cavern wall spurs my hooves faster, despite the sharp pains of my wounds.

The Underlord disapproved of my failure to bring Kinsey and has therefore shunned me from the keep. It's been slowly whispered across the wastelands that the Underlord is becoming trifling and mad. I never believed it until his actions this day.

Bringing my body into a full sprint towards the opposite side, I leap over the Grapner, who is starting to stir and land on the ledge they tossed me over earlier. Having been a knight as long as I have, I am aware of the secret tunnels that lead to the outside of the keep. With Kinsey in my embrace, we race across the flames that bellow around us and take a sharp left turn at the statue of the dismembered King before the Underlord. The sound of my hooves is quieted by the moss that overflows into the keep. A hidden trap door behind this statue is a secret not many are privy to. I, myself, had only stumbled upon it after a small sparring disagreement with one of the workers who feed the Grapner.

Seeing no one within the vicinity, we easily make our escape down the winding path through the keep that leads to the outside. Kinsey stirs in my embrace, not fully awake, but her arms wind up around my neck, giving her a better grip as she gets jostled with my trot.

The orange glow washes over both our bodies as we exit out the back of the keep. Once we reach a good cluster of trees, my hooves slow down to a stop. Turning back one last time to look upon the place I had called home for so many centuries, my eyes go over the details of the gaping maw that signify the exit point. The carving of the eyes that bare into your soul if one should dare to enter now stares at us in vengeance upon our escape.

Once I get my fill of the macabre sight, I turn around and start trotting ahead to scout out a good place to camp. My stamina and strength can only take us so far as the Underlord's lesser warriors' torture starts to slowly take its toll. The wounds inflicted upon my body start to throb in tune with my heartbeat as we continue to weave in and out of the clearing and cluster of trees. The Underlord is known to like these surrounding areas to be free of trees, so he can keep a close eye on anyone who dares to trespass on his lands.

Was paranoia the first sign of his madness? Many of us took it as vigilance on his part, being the lord over these lands. My mind cycles through the past memories trying to see if I can catch the times that showcased his slow descent into madness. The pain is overtaking my mind, and I can't seem to concentrate on any particular thought. We trot at a steady pace through another small grouping of trees until my mind reminds me of the landscape.

I wish to place Kinsey on my back. But in her state of unconsciousness, my fear is that she will fall and break a limb. Holding her it shall be then. Her warmth suffuses into mine, bringing weariness with it. The Underlord saw to my torture and stripping of my titles before they sentenced me to the Grapner. My body still feels raw in some of the areas his lesser warriors unleashed their wrath upon me, but the bloodline of my ancestors makes me hard to conquer. Her skin is soft, a welcome change to all the hell we've been through. She still does not stir despite the jostling I have to put her through on her trek across uneven terrain.

My mind wanders again under the orange haze of the sun. Where do I go from here? I have no one to serve; the Underlord has lost his loyalty from me. I am still unsure of his actual reasonings for his decision. Was it the fact that Kinsey was not brought forth? This slip of a female. What is it about her that makes him rage so? What secrets does she keep and how can she create such a reaction in a leader who is known for his cruel coldness and nonreaction?

I embrace her closer to my chest as we continue into more densely tree populated areas. Her skin is such a contrast to my own, more soft and intriguing. My years of being a knight to the King have not offered me the opportunity to court the opposite sex. The life one has in the wastelands is a life or death battle at all times. There isn't any opportunity for any pleasures of the flesh, at least not for me. Females are few and far between since the Underlord's takeover. Life was much different before his reign. Now, life seems to have slowly decayed, even more so in the wastelands than it did in the past.

The throbbing of my wounds brings me back to the present as I continue to tell my body to keep putting one hoof in front of the other to get us as far away from the keep as we possibly can.

An opening up ahead looks like the perfect place to stop and rest, it's what my weary body is telling me, anyway. It is just far enough from the keep that sentries would look in other areas first before trekking deeper into the woods. I am unsure of who commands this group of troops, but if it's one of the new commanders, they will not have the foresight to split the troops into multiple groups. No, they will have the ambition and greed to try and go in for the kill and ambush with their entire team with the hopes of seeking the reward of feminine flesh upon their success.

My legs almost give out by the time we make it to the designated spot. I control my limbs just enough to slowly lower Kinsey to the moss-covered ground; the wounds sending sharp pains, right before my body falls to the side, and the darkness consumes me. I hear her moan a little into the distance and my arms stretch out on instinct to seek her warmth. I need to keep her alive while I'm still alive. I need to...

CHAPTER ELEVEN

KINSEY

I wake up with warmth surrounding me. What the hell happened? My mind is groggy, the limbo between wakefulness and sleep. I hate this. Am I dreaming or am I awake?

I'm wandering down the halls. My mind is in a haze like I drank too much and also swallowed cotton balls. The room tilts as I walk, but I can't stop walking. I need to. I need to get out. The other person, she's walking towards me like a shadow along the walls. Is she really there, or a figment of my imagination? I feel myself lift my head up and the figure morphs into something asinine, but it can't be. I laugh. Why? It's funny though. She doesn't think so because she sneers her yellow teeth at me and starts to tackle me to the ground. My limbs move like I'm underwater. That's how my mind interprets it, anyway.

There's a pinch in my inner elbow, but I'm battling for my life. The pain doesn't register. Something is forcing my mouth open. Fuck this. I kick, punch, scream, and put everything into it, all my energy. I need to live. Fuck you! Get off me! Get the fuck away from me! All of you just leave me the hell alone!!

I awake with a jerk, and my heart is pounding. At least I think I'm awake because my eyes are open, right? How many times have I been fooled by this assumption, only to have woken up within another dream? The dream within a dream within a dream...a prisoner of my own mind.

I'm lying on my side; the ground is softer than what I remember. Where am I? The ticking, it's pounding in the back of my head. Is she going to get me? I start to struggle and cry when an arm wraps tightly around me. I let out a suffering breath, but it's not Erice's arm around me. This arm has exposed muscle and is bigger, heavier. What the? I feel so lost. Why did they hold me down like that? I feel so restrained. I can still feel the tightness in my limbs as I struggle to move but can't for some reason. My arms are stuck in their position of hugging my body. What the hell is happening to me? I turn around and bury my face into the warm embrace that's holding me. I want to cry. I want to scream. It's frustrating to feel like your mind is out of control and the thoughts that plague you in your waking state still want to confine you. It's suffocating!

My quiet sobs are pushed into the chest that holds me. I just want to feel something warm right now. Something that doesn't constrict me but lets me free. My arms loop around the shoulders before me by touch alone. I don't want to lift my head and face the world just yet. I need... I need...

When he holds me like this, I feel like I'm on top of the world. Nothing can come between us, nothing can separate us. The feeling of us becoming one is what I live for. My purpose. I love him so damn much. I need to feel more of him; I need him closer.

We're both lying on our sides facing one another in the quiet of the night, and I take the opportunity to lean in and smell his fresh scent. He smells of home, of safety. I need more. I lean in and lick up the side of his neck, feeling the pulse under my tongue and my body becomes hyper aware of our proximity. He's hot. It's making me hot. The leg I threw over his hip allows me to feel the hardness pressed between us. Our secret. The secret between us in the dark. I want it. I want it bad. I need it to take everything away. His breath starts to speed up the more I tease his skin with my tongue and nip his ear with my lips and teeth. I love driving him wild because he drives me insane all day long. I can't get him out of my mind. Fuck, I need it so bad and I squirm against him to let him know. Grinding my hot core against his erection.

"You're so fucking bad Kinsey."

"I need to feel your cock in me, please."

He groans into my ear as he proceeds to dry hump me with slow thrusts that only serve to tease than anything else. The friction sometimes hitting me right where I want it. My panties started to stick to me from how wet I'm becoming.

"Do you? You want my cock deep inside you, Kinsey?"

"Yes, I need to feel you cum inside of me. It's the only thing that dulls the burn. The need. Please!"

He groans even deeper into my ear as his hands perform quick movements to rip off my sleeping shorts and panties in one swoop. My intake of breath excites him even more when he nips my bottom lip as he pulls off his own coverings. His tongue distracts me for a few moments as it explores the recesses of my mouth as well as mind. I'm lost in this duel and my hunger only grows with every swipe. When his hot and hard shaft meets me between the legs, I automatically open up even wider for him, uncaring of how wanton it makes me. I just need him to dull the burn! The ache I have between my legs. I need him to fix it.

His thumb starts to travel down my stomach and navel in a slow and agonizing caress before it goes down far enough to my clit. Our lips continue to collide in the darkness, swallowing any of the noises that escape our mouths. When he starts to suck on my neck and circle my clit, I'm lost in a haze of lust and want. My hips thrust into his, hoping his cock, now slick with my juices, will just slip into me where it needs to be.

He forces me to flip over, dislodging our entwined limbs, pushing my face into the pillows to muffle the sound as his dick starts to slide between my folds in the slowest of rhythms to torture me again. He knows I love it and hate it at the same time. When one of his hands covers my mouth and the other comes down my front to raise my ass to his liking, his dick coated in my juices slides home in the most torturous of ways. One inch in, then out. A couple of inches in, then out. Dammit! Halfway in and so slowly out that I want to cry in frustration. When he feels my anger at his pace, he chuckles behind my head, licks the back of my neck and shoves himself all the way to the hilt, holding my mouth tightly in his palm so the scream is silenced in the night.

I find my tongue running a course along the thickly corded neck before me. I'm so hot and horny. The memory stirs something in me and now the ever-growing need is back. I need to fix my frustration. Now! I hate feeling this way. I need something in me to take the burn away to douse the emotions before I go up in flames.

The hand behind my back moves to fist my hair and force my head where he wants it to go. My tongue glides from his neck to his cheek across the jagged scar. He moans right before he takes my mouth against his, his tongue probing and seeking entrance. It's bigger than any tongue I've ever felt, but I don't let that fact stop me. The more we kiss, the closer we try to get to one another. His fist continues to hold a firm grip on my hair, causing spikes of pain every so often in my scalp, but it only spurs me on in this dance we're doing. Or maybe it's just me. I'm squirming, rubbing myself all over him like a cat in heat, with no shame. His teeth are sharp and nip at the meat of my lips, causing our kisses to have a metallic flavor mixed in. The mix of pleasure and pain is a heady one, and he's making me drunk off everything he's doing to me.

The other hand roams my ass, squeezing and gripping, sometimes sending small spikes of pain from the claws that prick my skin.

My hands come up to cradle his face, trying to bring our kisses even closer, even wetter. My eyes slowly open and I see blood-red ones staring right back at me. I wonder if he even closed his eyes once? Why does it make me hot knowing he's been watching all of my expressions during our kiss? Continuing to stare into his eyes, my kisses become desperate, needy. My tongue glides across his and his teeth, wanting to feel it cut me, wanting his tongue to soothe me. My right hand slowly caresses his scar from the bottom of his eye socket to the edge of his mouth.

His breathing changes and his kisses slow. We're no longer burning but simmering instead. The red in his eye changes a little, the color a little off before it becomes normal again. Isra is the one to stop the kiss. His fist in my hair slowly releases and begins to smooth it down instead. We're still staring at one another, laying on our sides. Remembering where I am, I give him a few chaste kisses along his scar before bringing myself up to sit and stretch my limbs, trying to pretend the kiss didn't happen. It didn't bother me but I have a strange feeling it made him uneasy towards the end.

I should hate him, but how can I hate someone in my same predicament now? We're both on our own.

Remembering all the times I would wake up to a fire with Erice, I begin to wander around looking for rocks to start creating our fire pit. I don't know how long we plan to stay here, but I remember Isra taking some wounds during the fight with the female before we exited the keep. The rustle of branches and leaves behind me tells me that Isra's getting up. I try to keep my back to him and ignore anything awkward between us as I start to rearrange the rocks I picked up into a circle on the ground. There is a lot of moss in this area versus the other areas I've camped at. Straightening up, I look around, trying to find a stick of some sort so I can remove the moss inside the circle.

Hands grab me from behind, and I gasp in surprise as I'm turned. Isra has me in an embrace and is staring at me intently.

"We cannot stay here. We have rested and must keep on going deeper into the wastelands, in case the Underlord sends more warriors under his command. The initial group was one of his newer ones, but it will only be a matter of time before he sends his more seasoned groups out to retrieve what he wishes to obtain. *You.*"

His red eyes are mesmerizing. I've never watched him talk without his helmet and armor before. The way the exposed muscles on his cheeks flex with the movement of his jaws and the way his scarred cheek flex is wrong but so right for him.

He clears his throat and my eyes snap to his from staring at his scar. He said the Underlord is after me. Why?

“I don’t understand. What does he want with me? I’m just a lost girl in this place. I’m just trying to find my way back home.” I’m sounding a little too much like Dorothy from the Wizard of Oz right about now. Maybe that’s the key. Maybe I need to find a witch? Some shoes? Erice made me moccasins. Does that count?

“This does not make any sense, Kinsey. There is no other place but here. What do you speak of?” He sounds confused but his face is unable to make the expression.

Didn’t that bastard Erice say the same thing? Do they really not know? Maybe they’re like me. I only knew of my own reality and then I ended up here. They probably only know of this place as their reality. This fact doesn't help me any though.

After a few moments, lost in thought, my eyes come back to Isra’s. His eyes have never left mine at all.

“We will begin our journey away from the keep. Ride with me and we will cover more ground.” That sounds like a plan. I mean, I heard what he said, and I knew what he was saying, but when he tossed my body over his back, I screamed.

He threw a glare my way, and I threw one back. What the hell, man?

Holding onto his waist, Isra starts a slow trot out of the cluster of trees and then bursts into a sprint, almost making me fall off. I must have been digging my nails into his rib cage, but he never let up on his pace.

This place is depressing. The orange glow is like somewhere between happy and sad. The smoke billowing out of the cracks on the ground like reverse tears or something crazy. At least, that's how my mind describes it.

We've been sprinting for quite some time, and it doesn't really look like we cover much ground. This is probably because everything looks the same. This barren wasteland of death. Sometimes I see things flying in the sky, reminding me of the creatures that caught up to me when I first found myself here. The sound that carries tells me they're really far away though, to even worry about them.

My grip starts to relax around his waist when his speed starts to slow. Peeking around the side, I see there's another cluster of dead looking trees up ahead. That must be our next stop. I really hope there's a pond or something there, I'm getting really thirsty.

Isra trots along and suddenly I hear something running towards us. Something hits Isra hard, and the momentum tosses me off his back onto the hard dusty ground beneath us. Luckily, he doesn't end up stomping over me because he's engaged in battle with something. More footsteps surround us, and before I can even stand up fully, a net or something is thrown over me. The weight of the net, though, is so heavy it knocks me back down and my forehead slams into the ground.

CHAPTER TWELVE

KINSEY

I come to and find myself on the ground, laying on my side. My forehead still kind of hurts. It's nightfall in the wastelands and there's a fire pit going. A good number of people or creatures are milling about. They carry the air of warriors or soldiers. They must be from the Underlord's keep. Crap, where's Isra?

The men around me look like some version of the undead. They look almost elven but their skin pallor is that of a corpse. This is becoming a common theme here. Their faces harbor a multitude of scars, some of which have peeled their skin away, but there isn't any actively seeping blood. Most of them have varying shades of gray hair. It reminds me of that first grey creature I ran into in this world. Amongst the orange hue of the environment, these guys look like they stepped right out of a black and white movie. Their ears are longer than human ears.

Getting myself up into sitting, I look around, trying to

find my centaur companion. We're in the cluster of trees that Isra was running towards. I guess the guys didn't want to camp out in the open in case other creatures came by.

Some branches snap behind me, making me jump and turn. Out from behind some tree trunks walks a male whose presence just takes up the air around me. He's bigger and bulkier than the other guys. His muscles make him look more menacing, more ruthless. His face is also much more skeletal, most of the skin having peeled back by now. His ears are like the others, longer than a human's. His exposed teeth showcase some fangs I didn't see on the other guys. What makes him different? I'm on edge because I don't know what to expect. I'm a prisoner, right? I need to get away from here.

He stops a yard from me, and we both continue to size each other up; it seems. His skin, instead of the dead pallor, is a deep, dusky grey blue with tattoos or scrollwork scattered all over. His hair is in short dreadlocks and ... his hands, he doesn't have any hands but instead two lethal looking flat blades that seem to have grown out of his very bones. Are my eyes deceiving me? They're shortening and changing shape before my very eyes until they become normal looking hands that are currently closed in fists. Holy mackerel.

My eyes shoot up to his as I bring myself up into standing so I won't feel so cornered. Always the prey.

"This is what the Underlord has tasked me to retrieve." He starts walking slowly to the side, and my eyes track his every movement. "I didn't believe my eyes, but here we stand. What does the Underlord want with a female such as yourself when there is plenty in his keep?" He has to be the leader because the moment he started speaking, the entire camp fell into a hush. Almost as if they are just waiting for his next command. What does he mean by a female like me?

He continues to circle me slowly, like a predator. Everyone here is a predator when compared to me. I'm going to have to figure out how to change this.

"I don't know why he wants me, I don't even know who he is."

"Hmmm."

The thing with these creatures I've run into is that none of them have discernable expressions because of the state of their face. It's like a recurring theme. Why is that?

When he circles back around me, he snaps an order in a language I can't understand and the other men start to busy themselves. What just happened?

He stands about a foot away from me now, finally revealing his height to me. He's tall. Everyone in this damn place is taller than I am. Despite standing a head taller than me, it's not his height that intimidates me, but the aura he gives off. He commands this group, which tells me a lot already. Insubordination also does not seem to be a problem for him.

"Where is Isra?" Where this courage is coming from, I don't know. But after that ticking head chick in the cavern, I suddenly feel a little less scared of him, commander of the undead elven army or not.

"The knight's been banished from the Underlord's keep. I made sure to keep him alive." At least there's that. One less worry. But how do I get back to him? We were both working to get away from the keep, and now this joker wants to bring me back.

"I need water. Please." I need to stall and figure something out. Maybe I can talk some sense into him if I get him away from his troops? Then what? I can't take him down physically. Look at the guy.

He stares at me for a few more moments before he turns and walks back towards the way he entered, deeper into the cluster of trees. The muscles on his back distract my thoughts. The other guys don't seem to notice or care.

They didn't chain me up like Isra. This is good. I'm staring at everything he's wearing in case I can snatch a weapon off him. A metal belt adorns his waist; the same medallions I saw on Grapner chick. I think that's what Isra called her. Must be a symbol of the Underlord. His back is all sinew and muscles, it's quite distracting watching it move like a walking weapon in itself. The tattoos emit a strange blue glow almost every time his muscles shift. Shit, that's right. His hands turn into giant blades. Maybe he doesn't even carry any extra on his body externally? Catching my eyes watching his ass move behind that warrior skirt of his, I have to consciously make my eyes continue to travel down.

A glint catches in the light. There! It's strapped to the wrap around his right calf. Okay, how am I supposed to get that? Think. Think.

I don't know how long we walk, but it's been over a good thirty minutes. The sounds of the other guys moving about do not even filter through the trees. A screech pierces the air, and my heart starts racing. Is it one of those red guys again? I actually run into his back since my mind is running with images of that red demon devouring the grey one.

My hands come up to steady myself and when I bring my head up, I realize it wasn't his back that I ran into. His eyes are unnerving because they look like caps over it, reflecting the orange hue of the wastelands.

"There is a pond that runs into a stream on the other side of this boulder. Do not think to escape." *Eesh.* This guy. Not like I can outrun him anyway...can I? I'm still thinking about that when I walk around the rock he's talking about. It's the biggest one here, coming up to my shoulder, and only provides a small sense of privacy. Better than nothing, I guess. My throat is feeling parched when I see the glistening liquid. It smells so fresh too. Man, when was the last time I drank anything?

Walking towards where the water starts to run into a stream, I cup some of the cool water in my hands and take a few refreshing drinks. Ahh, that tastes so good. I drink some more but try not to do it to the point where I might throw up. Looking at the water falling through my fingers, I think to myself that I might as well wash up a little. I splash some water over my face to wash any grime away and I automatically feel better, more awake. This is good. Now, to think of a plan, I need that knife.

When I walk around the large boulder, I realize some water splashed on my thin cotton dress. Dammit. Rubbing my hand over it and probably making it worse, I run into a hard chest again. *Ouch.*

The commander, or whoever it is, steadies me with his large grip on my arms. He's warm, despite looking like he's dead. I can't tell where he's staring, but I feel my nipples tightening from the wet shirt cooling in the air. I kind of slide myself out of his grasp and cross my arms over my chest. He hasn't moved. What is up with him? Okay, let's try something else.

"So, what is your name, anyway?" His head moves a fraction up with that. *I knew he was staring at my tits.*

"Ruspin. First Commander of the Underlord's army." Okay, that sounds really important, like a head honcho type. He can probably see my plan from a mile away.

"Ruspin, huh? Well, I'm Kinsey." His head tilts to the side and those eyes of his never tell me where they're roaming.

"Kinsey. What do you offer the Underlord? Why is he so adamant in retrieving you to send *me* when any of my warriors would do?" Well, that was out of the blue. Hitting me with the big guns.

"Your guess is as good as mine. I woke up one day and found myself in these wastelands. I'm just trying to get back home. I don't belong here. Hell, I don't even know how I got here."

"Or is that what you want me to think? Maybe you harbor skills unseen to the naked eye. What secrets do you keep, Kinsey?"

"I don't have any secrets. I told you what I know. I woke up one day, found myself in this wasteland and I never seem to be able to get home because of guys like you always foiling my attempts." Why doesn't anyone ever believe me? Do I have a lying face or something? I sure hope not, though that might help me...

"So, you harbor no ill will to our Underlord? You are not here to overthrow his kingdom? To take the throne for your own and make the people bow at your very..." His face looks down and then back up. "...little feet. To worship you as a dark queen over the wastelands." What the? Ain't nobody got time for that.

I take a step back because he started taking a step

forward. I know I shouldn't. This entices predators, doesn't it? That reminds me of the knife I want to steal from him that's currently too far away from my hands.

I must have backed up into the boulder because my back hit something hard and jagged. His nearness makes me tremble. His presence is all-consuming and sucks the air out of everything around him. My face is tilted up to stare at him so as to not show him my weakness too quickly, but when his chest touches mine, I turn my face to the side to break eye contact. It's too much.

His hand reaches up to grab my chin and force my face back to the middle. My breath hitches when I realize how close his face is to mine, we're almost kissing. I can feel the warmth of his exhales. Those eyes of his give nothing away, no matter how much I try to read them.

"The Underlord would destroy you quickly if what you say is true. Innocence has nothing to do with his will. He gets what he wants." His voice takes a lower tone. Or are my ears playing with me?

"What do I have to offer him? I'm nobody." The truth kind of sucks. But there it is.

He's still holding my face and forces my head to tilt as his skeletal face breathes across the crook of my neck in a slow sweep, sending tremors of a different kind through my body. I'm at his mercy. I can't take him on, not in a million years.

"On the contrary, you have a lot to offer." Do I dare? Should I make him let his guard down so I can steal his knife? What do I have to lose? Erice is gone, so is Isra. It's just me, and I can't survive out here without some sort of weapon.

"What do you want, Ruspin?" I let the statement hang

out there with a whisper. I hope this works because it has to. I have no other options.

"The Underlord is greedy with his possessions. Many of us left with the scraps of what he wants to throw out once he's done with it." His lack of a nose means he has to press his face even closer to me to even make any sort of contact. It's chilling and tantalizing all at once. Aren't all the males here? Knowing they can kill me any second.

"Is that what you want him to do with me? To use me up and wait until he's done to see if you can catch me then?" I gulp and mentally put my big girl panties on. "Why wait when you have me here, now?" I'm just going to throw the hook out and see if he takes the bait.

I bring my head back to center to face him again. Nothing is said, no one moves. We're staring at each other as our warm breaths mingle, that's how close we are. My eyes look into his and from this distance, I actually see it's not a covering but instead it's like the eyes of a fly and it's actually pretty intense, just like his energy.

"You are a temptation, aren't you? I can see why the Underlord wants you as his." The hand that was holding my chin starts to let go, and he moves his rough and calloused thumbpad slowly across my bottom lip. Wow, okay, who's tempting who here? My breathing is starting to pick up, along with my heart rate. His head tilts and starts to dip ever so slowly closer to my lips. Is this really happening? I have to let it right? I need to get his guard down to get his knife.

Before his mouth can touch mine, he spins around and blocks a blade coming right for him. I'm in shock. I was so lost in the moment; I didn't even hear anyone approaching us. I have some really sucky instincts and I'm not sure a blade would fix that fact.

I jump behind the boulder and peek out, only to see flashes of grey blue and pale red grey like meat that's been left out too long. Is that Erice?

In a flurry of slices and blocks, both Ruspin and Erice are wielding double swords. Most of the time Ruspin looks like he's winning but Erice would do something dirty and get the upper hand back.

Ruspin swings his arm blade upwards and Erice bends back just enough to miss getting cut, swinging his own blade from the right side. These two are well matched in strength and power and each time the blades strike one another, the loud metallic clang makes me grind my teeth together.

The sound of footsteps and boots crunching on branches coming towards us makes the fight turn even more frenzied. Erice knows he can't take on the whole troop and he's trying every dirty trick in the book to knock Ruspin on his back but is having a hard time achieving it.

The noise must have attracted other creatures in the area because a screech in the skies sounds much too close for comfort and the sound of another battle nearby entails. Erice smiles his signature shark smile as he continues to throw his blade in rapid speed against Ruspin. Since Erice's blades are thinner and lighter, his agility has an edge over Ruspin's arm blades. Erice distracts Ruspin with another barrage of swings and ducks to perform a quick swipe of his foot to topple Ruspin over.

I'm still staring at what just happened with my mouth hanging open when Erice jumps onto and over the boulder while sheathing his swords, bends down to throw me over his shoulder and starts running.

Is it always this way with him?

I still haven't forgiven him for his douche move when Isra came after me.

CHAPTER THIRTEEN

ERICE

The Rewsk used to be the main working class in these lands. Before the Underlord took over, the previous king cultivated a land rich with farming. We made the lands what it was; we fed the people.

The moment the Underlord took over was the moment the lands laid to waste. Every creature was forced to take up a sword and march with his war. His only goal to conquer everything in his path, for everything to fall to their knees before him.

When he's done with his use of you, he uses you for something else, chews you up, and spits you out to die.

This is what happened to my people. The once main working-class turning into mere soldiers, fodder for the kill, and then trash to be thrown back out into the wild to survive on their own. Many of us were annihilated during his warpath since he placed us right in the front of the line.

Those like me, who made it out, are now forced to live day to day for survival.

There is a rebellion brewing in the midst of it all. The whispers only floating along with the breeze in far distances from those who have gathered.

To see a commander of the Underlord's keep this far into the wastelands may mean he's on another warpath. I need to inform the others.

I may have to take the longer route back. That's what I tell myself as my hands caress my prize again. The longer path would distract the commander and his troops, put them off my trail instead of leading them back to the group.

Yes, this sounds like a fine plan. I missed this little bit. It's been boring without her.

The wastelands have shifted and changed lately, more desiccation cracks appearing where they haven't been. The smoke that billows become hotter with the increase of fissures.

Does this have anything to do with the Underlord and his moods? Does it speak of something impending?

We've passed a few groupings of trees beyond the expanse of plains, but there is better hidden ground to be found in the next batch. This will do. This will do. We need to be near water so we can last a while.

"What the hell, Erice? You can't just pop up and drop me like a hot potato whenever you feel like it!" Has she been speaking this whole time? Hopefully, she didn't say anything important because I didn't hear any of it.

Her legs start to kick me as I slow down to walk between the trees. One of those kicks hit me right in the stomach. This female's a wild one. I like it.

There is a small cave in this mossy clearing. But we'll be stopping to rest behind the cave instead, to use it as cover. Once we make it around the rocky side of the cave, I drop precious down to her feet. There she is. She looks like she's doing well. She staggers a little and I use it as an excuse to keep touching her. She is a soft one, isn't she? The taste of her folds still lingers on my tongue, even if it's been a week since I left her. I wonder if she'll let me have another taste?

Does that make me a bastard? I had to; it was the only way so that I could rescue her later. What good would I be to get caught with her? I'd be chained to the front of that keep like the rest of the fools who get caught in the middle of the Underlords rage.

Once she becomes steady on her feet, little bit's hand strikes out like a serpent, leaving a sting on my face. It makes me hot for her, this fire she gives me glimpses of. I wonder if I can get more out of her?

I shoot out my own hand and grab her neck and squeeze, making her mouth gape open for air, giving me the perfect opportunity for a reunion kiss.

She kicks, scratches and bites and I'm seduced.

She must miss me too.

When her knee makes it into my inserex, my breeding orifice, I feel my body preparing itself for some fun. Oh, I'm all for this kind of reunion. What a demanding little thing she is. I love it.

"Ugh! Erice! Get off me!" What's this? Surely she means 'get her off', something I'm more than glad to do. She does taste delicious.

When her little hands land on my face a few more times, I smile. Does she want to play like that? Her heartbeat starts to thrum faster on her neck, and I'm left a little confused. Why must it be so hard to read this female? She's the one that started this game.

"I do so enjoy your fondling of my orifice, little bit. Have you missed me as much as I've missed you?"

I didn't see the punch coming, but she continues to impress me. She slips away from me and my instinct to catch my prize starts to rise up again. For surely, she knows how I love to chase her.

"You are an asshole, Erice! You left me to get caught by that centaur. Do you know the kind of crap I ran into in that castle? I can still hear the ticking of that Grapner thing in my head sometimes when I close my eyes." Oh, she must really have some fight in her to survive that atrocity. She would make an excellent breeding partner. I can feel my inserex quivering in excitement.

"Did you hear me, Erice? Get your head out of your ass because I am not following you around anymore. I'm going to go look for Isra." My thoughts of rutting with little bit stops at the name of another male. What is this? How can she throw away what we have together?

"Isra, you say? And who pray tell, would this Isra be? Don't tell me it's that fool of a knight the king's commander got rid of?"

"What?! Got rid of? What are you talking about? You better not be fucking with me, Erice!" Her little fists start to attack my chest and I try to stifle my laugh. I want to kiss her. Her fury is beautiful even if it achieves nothing. I should rile her up more. It seems to make her touch me voluntarily.

"Tell me Erice! Have you seen him? Where is he?" Ah,

well, the attention was good while it lasted. I'll have to get rid of this Isra myself if she's acting this way.

"Last I saw, the good commander left his body to rot in the wasteland a mile or so east of here. But why do you want him when you have me to entertain you?"

"You're so full of it, Erice. Not everything is about you." I'd love to be full of it, full of her. My inserex starts to get wetter and when her eyes travel down my body, I shamelessly let her.

"Erice, good to see you and... not. I'll catch you later or never."

She leaves me.

My female leaves me.

I laugh at her audacity and let her think she can.

She'll never leave me because I'll never let her.

CHAPTER FOURTEEN

KINSEY

Screw him. I mean, I'm grateful Erice saved me from the troops, but he's still an ass and I don't trust him.

Walking around the cave, I see a pond of water in front of it. I'm sure this is the reason why we stopped here. Taking a few sips, I continue on my way.

When I make it out of the trees, I cover my eyes and look up. I think I'm heading east by the direction the sun is falling behind me. Well, no point in standing around. I never did get that knife from Ruspin.

Keeping an eye out for the sky creatures, I trudge along and keep a steady pace. My feet are still nicely covered by my moccasins, but I think it's getting close to becoming threadbare soon. I let out a sigh, thinking about the nice things Erice has done for me. But then I get fired up inside thinking about the asshole moves he's done too. *Ugh.*

Nothing out of the ordinary stands out in the plains area, so I trek towards another cluster of trees. I must have been walking for a good hour and my legs are feeling it. Finding a well-hidden spot to sit behind, I lower myself and bring my knees up. Laying my head back against a tree trunk, I let my eyes close for a bit.

A soft, almost inaudible footstep comes to my ear, making me jump up and look around. It better not be Erice, because I've had it with that guy.

"Kinsey?" His voice is broken, and he's limping from behind the trees. Isra looks like he took a beating he shouldn't have survived. My heart starts pounding a little because I'm really glad to see him. My survival rate just went up tenfold.

"Isra!" I tried to whisper yell so we don't attract unwanted attention.

I run toward him so he doesn't have to limp the whole way towards me, and he catches me mid-jump with a grunt. *Oops.*

"I thought I'd never see you again with the way everyone talks about you. From the commander to stupid Erice."

He chuckles and coughs up a bit. Poor thing.

"Well, if surviving some beatings gives me a greeting like this, I wouldn't mind going through a few more. Don't you know a knight of the Underlord doesn't die that easily?" My smile falls and my mind goes back to Giarsh. But they do fall Isra, I've seen it.

"Don't say that. I watched Erice chop up Giarsh like he was going to be potential dinner." My mouth curls in disgust at that thought, especially because I wouldn't put it past Erice at all.

The red in Isra's eyes turns a shade deeper, but he says nothing. Should I have not brought up Giarsh?

"What is past is past. How did you get away from the commander?"

"Erice decided to show up." His eyes change shade again, and I don't know what it means.

"The Rewsk that left you in my clutches? Well, no matter, we are together now. Both of us cannot return to the keep, so it's best we stick together." I'm glad we're on the same page.

He lets me slide down to my feet, not without wincing from some of his wounds.

"Do you need me to help clean your wounds? Are you going to get infected?" Isra gives me the weirdest look. What?

"The only way one becomes infected is through the will of the Underlord and his dark magic. One doesn't become infected through flesh wounds." He gives me another look, like he's considering something. "You really are not of our lands, are you?"

"I never lied." Finally, someone who believes me. You can't get infected here?

"Hmm. Well, our first task is to find water, and next a meal. We need to regain our energy for the trek we have ahead. We must keep our distance from the commander and his men."

"There was water back where I left Erice. We can go there but I really don't want to run into him again." Knowing the bastard, he'd probably just pop up out of the blue anyway to make me miserable for his own entertainment.

"Then that is where we shall go."

The trek back across the wasteland clearing doesn't seem as bad, perhaps because of the company.

Though Isra is limping, his pace matches with my brisk

one just fine. Before leaving the trees by where we reunited, Isra broke off large branches to use as spears. One for himself and one for me. How nice of him.

He was able to take down a small creature that scampered across our path along the way. It looks like a cross between a possum and a wolverine, but I'm so hungry by this point, I don't really care.

The sun is just going down ahead of us when we make it back to the cave. Just like Erice, Isra decides we should camp behind it to better hide our positions.

Isra is quick with making a roasting spit while I gathered stones to start on our fire pit. I wasn't able to discern which rocks would create good sparks to start a fire, but Isra had no problems. Sitting on the ground, watching him turn the meat, my mind drifts back into the past.

"Waylon, I need you to go out tonight." Our father sometimes likes to send him out doing who knows what. Waylon never tells me and I hate it when he's gone, because it means our father has me alone to himself.

"I just went out last week. How did we run out of money that fast?"

Slap!

"Don't talk back to me, boy. You do as I say. Get your ass out there. NOW!" Waylon looks back at me, sitting on the floor before he gets up to leave.

I'm shaking. I hate when I'm alone with him.

The sound of the front door closing reflects the sound of my heart shutting down, because I know what's coming.

"Get on your damn knees, Kinsey." I move to do as he says because if I don't he'll beat the crap out of me.

"That's right. That's exactly where you should always be." I'm

crying silently but he doesn't care. He just continues to unzip his pants, pull out his cock, and stroke it in front of my face in a slow rhythm.

"Open up, baby, take it all in. That's it. That's a good girl."

Why my mind even thinks about that, I have no clue. But it makes me miss my brother badly. I wonder if he's doing okay without me? The sound of the fire starts to soothe me and I feel my eyes drifting close every now and again as I wait for the food to cook. The sizzle of the fat melting into the fire creates a sort of lullaby.

"Hey, Kinsey! Do you want to go camping with me?"

"I've never been camping! Mom! Can I go? Can I go?" I look over to my mother sitting in the front yard with grandma in their lawn chairs. Mom is so beautiful in her dress, sitting in the sun.

"Camping with who, honey?"

"With David from across the street. He asked me to go camping with him!" David is older than me and I'm so excited to get invited! I'm ten now and that should be old enough to go camping.

"Where are you guys planning to go camping?" David blushes and rubs the back of his head.

"We call it camping but it's just in the backyard." I don't care. I'm so excited! I also have been building a small crush for David secretly.

"Oh, that's fine then." Yes! "As long as your brother Waylon comes too." Oh no.

"Yea, that's totally fine. He can come. We'll have a good time." David sends me a dimpled smile and I internally sigh and squeal but on the outside, I try to keep a straight face in front of my mother. I was hoping I could sneak my first kiss with David if we were alone. But now Waylon's coming.

Speak of the devil. I feel Waylon throw his arm over my shoulder as he greets David with the usual bro greeting of that weird handshake they do.

"So, we're camping, huh?" Waylon nudges me and I shove him back. "I'm down for that."

Of course, he is.

I miss home, even if home sucked later.

How do I get back?

CHAPTER FIFTEEN

KINSEY

Something is touching me softly. Opening up my eyes, I find Isra's face really close to mine, his hands grazing my cheek. My mind is still groggy, and I'm trying to figure out how we ended up in this position. I fell asleep by the fire after eating the meat he roasted. That's right.

"Good morning." My voice is croaking from the lack of water. I clear my throat and bring myself to sitting to stretch all the kinks out. How did I ever think camping was fun? I'm getting my fill of it now.

Isra brings his horse body up into a half-lying position that allows his top body to come up to my similar position. He hasn't said anything yet.

We stare at each other for a few moments, and I clear my throat before turning away to hide my burning cheeks. It's a bit awkward, being stared at so intently. I didn't forget what happened the last time we rested together. I was caught in the heat of the moment from the tail end of the dream. But the dream wasn't a dream, was it? It was a memory. Now my cheeks feel even hotter.

"We should get going. Get farther away from the guys coming after us." I clear my throat again. Man, I need some water. At that, Isra gets up on his hooves.

Am I going to be trapped in this world forever? If I don't understand how I got here, how can I even begin to figure out how to get home?

"There are whispers in the wind of a rebellion against the Underlord. We should find them to seek sanctuary." That's a sound plan. Would they accept outsiders like us, though? Especially Isra, who used to be a knight.

"Isra, would they take you in knowing who you are?" Looking over him, I notice his body heals exceptionally fast. The superficial wounds are gone and the deeper ones look on their way there. Amazing. Come to think of it, I don't think I feel the pain of the one on my calf anymore. That makes my mood sour, thinking of stinking Erice and his games.

"I am unsure, but we have no other alternatives. Come, let us refresh ourselves before we leave camp."

These moccasins are really on their last leg. Should I toss them? This dress of mine is pretty thin too. How did I end up in this place with an outfit like this, anyhow?

We drink our fill and wash our faces. When I stand up and start straightening my dress, I noticed I wet the top of my dress again. Dang it.

I yelp when Isra grabs me under the arms and lifts me up, my arms automatically going around his shoulders to hold on.

He has a look I can't decipher on his face.

"Kinsey, when we reach sanctuary, will you remain by my side?" Is this a simple question or is he asking me something more? My heart kind of feels full. What a lonely existence he would have if he was the only centaur cast out here, essentially banished.

"We'll stick together until we get somewhere safe. But I need to find a way home." He doesn't respond to that but instead just throws me onto his back. After picking up his spear, I pat his side as we walk out of our campgrounds.

I have no idea if he knows where he's going, but I don't say anything because it's not like I'm any better. We're trotting along when an arrow lands right beside us, making Isra rear up on his hind legs, almost tossing me off.

Shit.

The sound of footsteps stampeding towards us can be heard and Isra goes into a sprint. He still has his spear, and it reminds me that I forgot mine by the waters. A shadow looms over us and when I turn to look, I see Ruspin mid-jump about to land on Isra's back. Holy mackerel, this guy is good. I pat Isra's side rapidly and he bursts into another sprint. The commander lands right behind us and is running right on our heels.

The sounds of swords swishing come from the left and behind us. What the hell, how did the warriors gain on us that fast? I sneak a peek back, and I can't believe my eyes. Erice is in another sword battle with Ruspin. How does he keep popping in and out?

Isra enters a grouping of trees and is zig-zagging all over the place. We're just about to pass a large boulder when someone knocks me off his back. My body hits a few branches and I try to fall the rest of the way into a roll to try and soften the blow. By the time my head stops spinning and I stand up to look around, I see Erice on Isra with both his swords drawn. My mind flashes back to Giarsh and I'm panicking. He can't! Isra is all I have!

My eyes zone in on one of the broken branches from my fall and with a courage I didn't know I had, I pick one up and throw it at Erice, who is still on Isra's back. It misses the mark, of course, but it did get his attention. He points his shark smile at me and jumps off Isra's back and runs right towards me. Oh hell no, not again!

I quickly bend down to grab another broken branch to use as a makeshift weapon and point it right at him. Why does he look like that? Like he's excited at the prospect.

"Always the warm welcome, little bit. I missed you too. If you're done playing with the knight, I think it's time we go home." What in the world? He is out of his damn mind.

I shove the branch forward and his sword slices off a chunk. Damn, that was a bad plan. I'm still trying to figure out what I'm going to do next when Isra comes up behind Erice, ducks under one of his swings, and picks him up to throw him against a tree. The thud makes me wince. But it had to be done. Erice is a damn menace.

Erice shakes himself a little in a crouched position and jumps right back into the fray with Isra. I don't know how he's going to block the sword swings, since he doesn't have any armor anymore since we left the keep.

Erice leaps into the air and is about to slice down with his sword when another body slams into him. *This is bad.* The troops must have caught up with us. I'm looking around, frantic, but no one else is here but the new guy. The new guy being Ruspin, it has to be.

Erice and Ruspin go at it much more aggressively than Erice and Isra. My mouth is hanging open with how hard they're swinging their blades and jumping to avoid the other person's swing. They're almost a match for skill and it puts me on pins and needles to watch them because I don't know who's going to make it out of this fight.

My body gets slammed a little, but it's Isra who is trotting off with me in his arms. He's bleeding in some places but doesn't look too worse for wear. The sounds of metal clashing get lighter and lighter the further out we ride. Twining my arms around his shoulders, I bury my face into Isra's body as he repositions his arms to hold me bridal style.

We both get knocked down to the ground during our run across the open, and I can hear Isra grunting in another fight. How did they catch up so fast?

When I brush the dust off my face, I see Erice attacking Isra and Ruspin attacking Erice. This is going to be a shit show. What do I do? Do I save myself and run? It's not like I can jump into the fray between these three guys going at it.

I decide to run, good idea or not. I only make it a few yards when I'm tackled into the ground by a heavy body. I struggle the best I can and turn to punch him in the face, but his hand catches it before it can make contact. Ruspin is staring at me intently while he's pinning my body down. We're both breathing hard and my mind is getting mixed messages because the line between sexual tension and fear is becoming really thin by the moment.

His face inches closer to mine, but he never makes it all the way because he jumps off me to turn and block a hit from Erice behind him.

"Now, now. I know everyone likes my little bit. But you

males forget who she belongs to." How does Erice continue to talk calmly while they're both fighting to their deaths? I scamper back like a crab and jump into standing, looking everywhere for Isra.

He's gone. Where is he? Did he get killed? What? What do I do now?

Watching the two before me go at it again, I turn and run. I don't know where I'm going, but I'm getting away from these two. I jump a few fallen logs and dried skulls before I hear a screech in the distance. Crap! I increase the speed of my sprint and hope I can find another cluster of trees before whatever is in the air sees me.

I can actually feel the air whooshing from the creature's descent to the ground, and I scream. Please legs, please don't fail me now. I try to run zig-zag and all crazy directions to put whatever it is off my trail, but the feeling of air shifting is still close enough to move my hair. One of my moccasins takes this very moment to rip apart from the bottom and I trip to the ground with my hands, shooting out to try and stop the fall. My hands get scraped up, but I can barely feel it because I turn to face my death and another scream is lodged in my throat.

Ruspin's blade has sliced through the red beast's neck from below and Erice's blade has sliced through from its back. My heart rate still hasn't slowed, even when the boys continue to slice and dice from either side and finally decapitate the creature. Its head hits the ground with a very wet thump and it rolls until it comes right next to my foot. I freak out with its proximity in case it can still bite me, jump up, scream, and kick it like a damn soccer ball.

Erice is still standing on the body of the beast and lets out a booming laugh.

But then Ruspin does too. I growl and start walking away from the madness towards the direction I was running anyway.

“Hold on, little bit.” Erice grabs my arm and twirls me towards him. I twirl with a slap to his face. This fucker smiles because he loves this shit. He loves it so much; he attacks me with a kiss I didn’t see coming. I’m kicking and scratching and he just moans into my mouth. He’s suddenly pulled off me, and Ruspin has him by the throat with one hand.

The smile never leaves his face. I don’t wait and see what happens because I take the opportunity to turn and run.

CHAPTER SIXTEEN

RUSPIN

This infuriating male is getting on my last nerve. Vagabond of the wastelands. I haven't run across a Rewsk in a long time but his days may be numbered because my hands still itch to kill.

I let the little female run, let her think she's getting away. She ignites something within me, a fire that hasn't burned before. It's an uneasy feeling but I come to find that I'm starting to enjoy it when it arises. I'll find her again after I'm done with this male.

He smiles and bares his teeth at me, putting me on edge. This wretched creature ignites a whole different feeling in me. One that grates me.

His agility is impressive but my need to exact a bloodbath, even more. We clash our swords again, coming in from above and below. The clang of metal on metal fuels my rage. The grunts he makes pumps my blood. We match each other in strength, but this creature's penchant to fight dirty makes me put more strength into my swings. Sparks fly and the smell of male and sweat enters my nostrils, the adrenaline heightening my senses for the battle. With quick movements, I finally disarm him but he is quick with his jump back and roll to pick his weapon back up. I tire of this game we play and I need to find the female before she gets too far away.

Taking the few steps I need towards him, I bring my blade up from below and the side, the sound of it cutting the air loud in my ears, forcing his weapons from his grasp. His grunt and hiss make me smile as my blades retract back into my hands. I leap and bring all of my weight down on him, taking him to the ground.

The dust surrounds us in our frenzy, blinding us momentarily, the smell of earth and sweat prominent with how close our bodies are.

Our fists land blows on each other with malice and speed. I have him pinned under me in submission, but his claws rake my face, the warmth of the blood trickling down, tickling me...the warm wetness exciting me. We struggle in a battle of dominance and tangle of limbs when he finds a way to force both our bodies to our sides, ripping my warrior cover from my hips with a hard snap. The sting barely registers. A swift kick to his ankles from my position and a few fists to the face, and I'm able to push my forearm into his neck to subdue his fight back onto his back with a hard grunt from both of us. Our current position allows me to feel his orifice slick with want, and my phallus responds accordingly, not caring who's beneath me. Fight and lust are one and the same when warriors are in battle. The adrenaline-fueling arousal in the most inopportune times, especially for one such as me.

The need to dominate this wretched menace takes hold of me and my instincts lead me to lean in and bite down on his neck to assert my position, the sound of his skin popping making me ravenous. When the blood explodes into my mouth, I pull in a big gulp and the taste makes my mind go into a craze. My body moves on its own, thrusting with each suck, as I continue to pull in and swallow mouthfuls of Rewsk blood.

He moans and starts undulating beneath me, sliding our core together, teasingly pulling the head of my phallus in every so often. But the need to dominate consumes my thoughts and I unlatch my mouth to growl while pushing harder with my forearm onto his neck, choking him more right before I invade his center with my hard cock. It slides in with ease as the heathen beneath me has already been emitting fluids since our tumble on the ground. The warm wetness surrounds my cock, making it almost vibrate with eagerness. We both start to struggle and fight once more, his fists landing a few blows on my face, the sounds of groans and grunts mixing together. My free hand grabs and pins one of his to the ground while I take another bite and suck of his blood. I pound my cock into him with force to keep him from moving, but the more I suck, the more he starts to fuck me from below.

"You like that, don't you, commander? Sucking me in." His words shouldn't ensnare me, but they do, and I do suck more of his blood in large swallows. This wasteland rat needs to be eliminated.

The push and pull drive me higher and higher. With

another pull of blood and a lapse in judgment, the Rewsk under me slips his hands free to circle my throat, pulling my mouth from his shoulder, causing a jagged wound. He continues to smile and bare his teeth while I continue my invasion of his center. One of his hands and claws slashes across my chest, the sting of pain enhancing my arousal and making my abs and balls tense up towards an inevitable climax fast approaching.

"Looks like you're wet for me." His wide smile grates on my nerves.

My thrusts become erratic and aggressive as I pound him into the hard ground, the dust starting to surround us again before finally letting out a growl upon my release. The Rewsk growls back with just as much force as his orifice floods even more with his own fluids, his grips loosening ever so slightly. I jump back and away from his body to allow me enough room to swing my arm blade down right where he lays. This ends now!

His agility is uncanny as he turns his body just in time and twists to grab and swing his own blade at me. I tire of these petty games he plays and come in for another killing blow. He parries my hit with both of his blades crossed, sparks flying, and the one that takes the brunt of the hit breaks in two. The moment my eyes watch the blade fall was the moment he takes advantage of my inattention. He shoves his foot into my stomach with all of his weight, making me double over with a grunt, and proceeds to jump over me to escape.

I scream into the skies right before I charge after him.

CHAPTER SEVENTEEN

KINSEY

I'm lost. Dammit! I was weaving through the trees, trying to put the guys off my trail, hoping if they are following me by scent or tracking my footsteps, they'll get just as lost as I am.

Well, so much for that plan. Am I going around in circles? All these trees look the same! The smell of the smoke billowing from the cracks in the clearing comes all the way here, making me unable to use my sense of smell to see if I'm on a different path.

I'm tired and this stupid moccasin flapping with every step like it's trying to talk to me is beyond saving. Unwrapping my right foot, I throw the shoe with all my frustration, hitting a nearby rock with a sad thump. Okay, I need to think. I'm on my own. Isra and I were heading west, I think. I need to get out of this cluster of trees to see where the sun is in the sky. Okay, just choose a direction.

I start to stomp forward, crunching some dead grass and

small twigs with my moccasin-covered foot when the hairs on the back of my neck go up. The hair on my head shifts a little. Was that breeze a normal breeze or something else? I was so busy stomping in frustration; I didn't hear anything around me. Stupid Kinsey. I need a better sense of my surroundings. This is exactly why I wanted to be traveling with Isra!

Something touches my shoeless ankle, and I yelp and jump. I kick it and try to stomp on it, but it moves too fast. I'm actually chasing it a few steps to try and step on it again when I'm caught in a strong embrace. He smells of dust, sweat, and something else I can't put my finger on.

"So easily lured, precious. Have no worries, we're back together now. I think I deserve a little something for always winning this game we play, don't you?" I swear I can never shake him. He's like gum stuck on your shoe and now I'm one shoe down. His hug is so tight with my arms pinned to the side that I can't do anything but glare at his stupid face.

He chuckles and starts to smile his signature smile right before he sticks out his tongue and licks my cheek like an animal. Ugh! My face must be saying what's on my mind because he lets out a laugh with his head thrown back this time. I notice a really ugly and gnarly jagged wound on one of his shoulders and wince in sympathy. How does he even go on like it's nothing?

"Erice, you should look at that." When he bends his neck back down towards me, blood oozes from the wound and I can't help but watch it drip down his chest.

"Would you like a closer look, little bit? A taste? How about a trade, hmm? A taste for a taste."

"Put me down. Now. I'm tired of your games; I have places I need to be."

He sneaks in a wet lick across my lips and puts me down. I wipe them with the back of my hand and start stomping away. I can hear his footsteps right behind me and feel his stupid tapeworm tail caress my shoeless ankle every now and again.

The more I walk, the more I realize there's a damp spot on the front of my dress. What the hell? I stop and Erice pretends to run into my back, his hands caressing my arms and his tail trying to creep up my thigh.

"Stop that! Why is my dress wet?" I turn around and look down at his crotch. This is that smell. It's the smell of sex, but more pungent, more musky, more something. How did he even have the time to stop for a quickie, and why does my chest feel like this? Why am I feeling upset about it?

"Now, now, little bit. No need to fret. The commander and I had to ... settle our differences." What? The commander...

"I do like this look on you, precious. Maybe the commander and I need to have a go more often if you continue to get all jealous like this. I do so enjoy your attention. I *can* make it all better." What? Jealous? Me? I-I-I don't know if I'm jealous of Erice or the commander, and that fact just makes me even angrier.

Why should I care? Fuck Erice.

I choose to ignore him, turn, and keep on walking. My toes squelch on something wet on the moss and I close my eyes and breathe hard out my nostrils. Disgusting!

Erice chuckles and throws me over his shoulder while I'm standing there on one leg, trying to figure out how to proceed. I let him because let's be real here. I can't do this on my own. I do notice that one of the hilts of his blades looks different than the other. I thought he had matching ones?

Erice walks briskly and jumps over a few logs, jostling me and making my stomach hurt a bit. It's a good thing I haven't eaten in a while because I would probably be throwing up by now.

We end up walking up a hill and descend back down somewhere. I can't tell since I'm only seeing the view from the rear. Finally, after who knows how long. But my head is getting woozy from the blood flow, Erice slides me down his body ever so slowly. I'm sure he's trying to be seductive, but I feel too light-headed to care. I almost fall backward, but Erice holds onto my waist and lets me bend back halfway, like he's dipping me in a dance.

I realize both of my feet are wet and look down to see we're at the edge of a river. Erice leans in and sniffs me between my breasts, making me jolt to attention. This guy and his liberties!

"Erice, please! Can you not be... Be yourself for a minute!" His chuckle vibrates my breasts, and it makes my nipples peak. He continues to rub his face against them and hums again. When his mouth closes over one of my nipples over my dress, I gasp and shove him.

What I didn't count on was him letting me fall and splash into the river, soaking me from head to toe. Ugh! My foot's clean but now I'm all wet!

I growl and jump at him, throwing my fists because he gets on my nerves! What does he do? He laughs and then pretends to fall down onto his back, making me land on top of him. Him and his games! I jump off him and start to wring as much water as I can out of my dress and my hair. It doesn't help, but I like to pretend it does just so I can simmer in my anger a little longer at this bastard.

I hear a splash, and more water hits me in the back. I fucking scream. I don't care who is following us because I can't take him anymore!

I bend down and grab a rock because I'm about to throw this right in his fucking face, but when I turn, I'm caught off guard. Erice's back is to me. He looks like he's washing himself, but he also looks like he's jerking off. How can that even be possible when he doesn't have a dick? What the hell is he doing?

I throw the rock at the back of his head anyway, because I'm tired of caring. It hits its mark, and I turn to stomp away. A few yards in, I bend down and throw my last moccasin against the ground with a really wet squelch. So much for that.

I weave through some trees and I have no idea where I'm at, but I keep walking anyway. After a few moments, I somehow manage to turn myself around and there's Erice, standing with his arms crossed like he was just waiting for me to return. Heck, he's even still wet. Damn him! Damn this place!

Erice starts to smile and crooks his finger in a come hither motion. *Hell no.* I start backing up. He starts walking forward. I turn to run and he grabs me from behind, making us both fall but with him landing on his back. I struggle to escape by crawling off his body towards his legs, but instead of making it anywhere, Erice's arms band around my body and tighten to almost the point of pain, making me stop and squeak. My dress is still wet, and now twisted and riding up my body. The only reason I realize this is because I become very aware of his hot breath right between my legs.

I hate the guy, I really do, he's such a damn jerkface, but when his hot wet tongue starts to slowly slide against my folds all the way up to my back entrance, I shiver. He's way too good with that tongue of his. I've stopped struggling and he must realize this too, because he chuckles into my pussy and starts to dip his tongue in like he owns the damn thing. I moan into his hip. I can't help it. Damn him. His tongue starts to reach and play with my clit, going back and forth from licking seductively to dipping it inside me like the nasty creature he is.

His arms release their hold on me and start to caress my body towards my ass. It makes me shiver and gives me goosebumps the way he seems to revere his touches. When both of his large hands reach my ass, he grips them hard and forces them apart right before his overly large black tongue dips into my pussy again and again like a hard cock thrusting into me, a cock with very dynamic muscles to hit places inside me I didn't know existed.

My hips are starting a steady dance and his tonguing becomes more aggressive. Every time my pussy starts to show any sign of tensing towards a climax, he slows his ministrations down torturously. I'm shamelessly grinding into his face at this point, using his chin to hit my clit as his tongue continues to poke and prod and fucking claim my pussy.

I hate the way he makes me feel. I hate that I love him when he's like this. Less of a bastard and more of a giver. He gives really, really good pussy licking. But you know what? Two can play at this game. With my head still leaning on his left hip, my right hand starts to glide over his opening, gliding past my hand to my wrist. I don't penetrate him just yet because this fucker has teased me way too much. It's time to give him a taste of his own medicine.

I keep passing my hand to and fro in the slowest of motions while my hips continue to thrust into his face. When he moans into my pussy, I dip just my middle finger into his opening. It's wet, slimy, and hot. The heat reminds me of his tongue in my opening, and I can feel myself starting to throb at the thought. This shouldn't turn me on like this.

One finger turns into two and suddenly it's Erice thrusting towards my hand, seeking more. *How do you like it, huh?*

"Kinsey..." He mumbles my name into my pussy, and it does something to me. Knowing I have a sort of control over him like this. It's empowering in a land where I feel so damn helpless all the time.

I stick my hand into his folds vertically up to my knuckles and pull out. He's so hot and wet inside. I choose to put my whole hand into his opening in the next pass and spread all my fingers inside him. This makes him start to lick and nip at my pussy with fervor. We continue this give and take, both of us thrusting into each other until I'm shoving my hand all the way up half my forearm. Fuck, I think I'm pounding into him like I'm punching him on the inside when all my clit grinding on his chin finally puts me over the edge and I stifle my moan by biting into his hip and writhe with pleasure. I forget him for a moment and continue to pant against his hip but when the climax starts to die down; I go back to fisting Erice like I'm pissed at him, because really, I am. He's always putting me in these strange predicaments, popping in and out of my life like he has the right to.

After a few more strokes, Erice is grinding himself into my arm and lets out a muffled growl into my pussy. His opening starts to squelch with more of his fluids and honestly at this point, I can't even find it in myself to be disgusted because this is just Erice. The nasty fucker.

I pull my hand out and place it over his hole like I'm covering it from the elements when Erice continues to lick all my juices off me like a starving man. Why does he have to be so good at that?

When he's done, he gently pushes me aside onto my back, turns around himself, and nuzzles into my neck on top of me like we're fucking cuddle buddies. It's okay though because the breeze started to pick up a while back and now that we're not in the middle of our activity session, it's getting a little chilly. Erice's body blocks most of the wind and his warmth starts to seep into my weary bones, causing my eyes to slowly fall letting the darkness embrace me.

CHAPTER EIGHTEEN

KINSEY

I wake up to the warmth of a fire near me. It's still nightfall. I felt like I've been sleeping forever. Has it really only been a short nap?

Sitting up, I rub my eyes and look around. What the hell? Wasn't there a river here? Where did it go? I turn around and I swear this is a whole different place. Where the hell is Erice?

Speak of the devil. Here he is swaggering back into the camp. But *is* this our camp?

"Where did the river go?"

"Ah, little bit. You were so amazed by my ministrations of your body it seemed it needed more sleep than usual." He can never give me a straight answer or a serious one.

"What are you talking about? Speak straight." He laughs and smiles at me. It's at this moment I notice he's got another water bladder and something hanging behind him.

"You were in such a deep sleep, you didn't even feel me

pick you up and move camp. It's the next day already, precious." What. In. The. World? I don't remember being a deep sleeper. How can this be?

The floor creeks and my eyes shoot open. No, not again.

When the door slams open, my father grabs me and takes me into the living room. He smells of alcohol and isn't walking straight. He throws me over the arm of the couch and rips my sleeping shorts and panties down so hard it burns my thighs like a scrape. The sound of his zipper makes my heart pound. No matter how many times it happens, it never dulls the fear. This is why I've become such a light sleeper, barely getting the rest I need for my body.

"That's impossible. I'm not a deep sleeper."

Erice walks over to me and holds my face with his hands while his tail starts to wrap around one of my legs.

"Well, little bit, you were then. You were so peaceful; I didn't want to wake you." Why is he like this? Why is he hot and cold all the time? Sometimes he's sweet. Sometimes he's an asshole who slices your calf and leaves you to die.

He steps back a couple of paces and brings whatever he has slung over his back to the front. There's some sort of furry creature that resembles a jackrabbit if it went through radiation and started to mutate into a dog, and something else furry I can't comprehend.

Erice bends down and removes two furry things from the line they're all attached to. Suddenly grabbing my foot, I almost topple over if I didn't hang onto his shoulders. I slap the back of his head for good measure because I hate this shit. He never tells me any of his plans.

"Relax, little bit. Relax."

When he's done putting on my first moccasin, he grabs

my other foot and does the same. I'm telling you he gives me whiplash. I don't know whether I should hate him or hug him. Ugh.

When he stands back up, he's looking smug as heck, like he's waiting for something. I look back down to my feet and start to tear up, but I hold it in. I don't want him to see me weak like this. The bastard would just take advantage of it.

"Kinsey, you're looking beautiful today." My face heats up and I try my best not to smile.

"Thank you, David." His flirtation has been increasing lately but despite that, it still makes me blush like the first time.

"She looks fucking beautiful every day, you asshole." Waylon punches David in the shoulder and his face is fierce. Not this again!

"That's what I fucking meant. Damn, lay off." Waylon, despite being around a similar age to David, hit a growth spurt this past summer and now stands half a head taller than David at just over six feet tall. I don't know what father has him do when he gets sent out, but he's been putting on muscle and coming home with cuts and bruises sometimes.

"What you need to do is lay off my sister."

"Just chill, ain't no crime with paying a lovely lady with a compliment." I don't think Waylon knows about the kiss he stole the other day.

Waylon shoves him again before growling in his face. "She's not even sixteen yet. Keep. Away. From my sister."

When did they begin to go from close friends to this? It seemed everything changed since David gave me a small gift and a peck on the cheek. I didn't see Waylon around the corner, watching us. By the time I spotted him, he was already walking away.

Nothing nice ever lasts. I can't let my walls down with

Erice. He would probably throw me under a bus if he had to save himself. I need to remind myself of this fact before I let all his nice moments make me weak.

"Thanks," I mumble as I step away from him.

"You must be hungry. I made you something earlier, but you were still sleeping. I kept it for you." This sweet bastard hands me something that makes my mouth water. It still smells delicious, like grilled chicken, and my stomach chooses that moment to rumble. Giving him a quick thanks, I start devouring it, licking my fingers at the end. A groan comes out of him and when I turn to look, he's rubbing his hand over his stomach down towards his opening without touching the opening itself. This dude gets aroused by anything.

"Alright then. Let us head up before the sun comes up. It will take a few hours by foot but we should get to our destination before the sun is too high in the sky." Wiping my hands on my dress, I look at the threadbare material. I hope they have extra clothes I can have when we get there. This dress is almost see-through by this point.

Just like Erice said, it took us a few hours on foot with a rest break to reach what looks like a dilapidated town made from scavenged materials.

There are two sentries or something that stand guard at the front. I can't see the details from this distance too well. I'm trudging along slightly behind Erice.

"You decided to come back to us, hey? Had enough of the bullshit out there, Erice?"

"Now, now fellas. I just had to go back for something I lost."

"Color me curious, Rewsk. What would a wasteland rat

like you lose? More than likely, it's something you stole." The two sentries laugh and it's a baritone sound. We've stopped walking now, and I put a hand on Erice's back to peek out a little. I don't know what I'm dealing with. Better the devil you know and all that.

The guy I can fully see has a helmet of sorts that has antlers poking out of the sides. It doesn't end there though. There are also tusks attached to this helmet that jut out from the side of his face. His smile is disturbingly large and menacing, especially since the helmet covers half down his face over his eyes. Maybe he doesn't have eyes. His gums look like they're receding back, exposing more teeth than necessary. His body reminds me of an orc, at least like the ones in David's video games, olive skin tone and all. His hair pokes out the back in a long straight black ponytail of sorts. His large muscular arms are crossed, exposing the weapons he carries on his hip belt. Two axs. Around his neck is a necklace of fangs that looks much too large for my comfort.

When Erice pulls his swords out from his sheaths, the hair on the back of my neck stands up. I also kick him right in the ass because the move could have sliced my damn face off! He never tells me a damn thing. He doesn't even flinch. Instead, his tail just wraps around my ankle and caresses it.

"Now, now. We'll play later." This fool pats me on the arm from behind like he's giving me a lover's promise. "First, I need to let these fine gentlemen know that I worked hard to get you back and that you belong to me." I'm not sure if I should be flattered or if I should slap him upside the head for being so damn cocky about us. But it's just like Erice to be declaring something like that in front of everyone. I shake my head, even if he can't see it.

"Worked hard? What are you hiding? Is it a female?" I can literally hear one of the guys sniffing the air and snorting. This place.

"It doesn't smell male, it must be. How did you find one out this far? Has the Underlord been getting rid of his stash, then?" What the hell?

"No, it doesn't smell like his usual cast-offs. This one is different." I don't think I smell that bad. I sniff under my arms just to make sure.

More snorting and grunting happen. I'm pinching the bridge of my nose between my eyes because these cannot possibly be the people to give us safe sanctuary. I don't feel safe at all.

My hair gets blown in front of my face when Erice, in a flash, starts swinging his sword and sweeping the legs of both these sentries, landing them on their asses. I swear, when we get alone I'm going to chew Erice a new one. He cannot go around doing this all the time. How the hell are we supposed to feel safe and find peace here?

"Uh.. sorry about that, guys. Erice is just...Erice. We come in peace and hope you can give us sanctuary? The Underlord has sent out some men to come after me." I'm nervously trying to smile and wave to ease the tension Erice created. The guy I didn't get a peek of looks up at me with the face of a damn anteater. He's covered in hair and has four arms. But it doesn't end there. His feet are hooves. I am so confused right now. He has a chest strap that looks like Erice's crisscrossed one but instead of swords, it's two short spears that peek out.

That brings me back to our current situation. What is

Erice doing beating up the sentries? We need to find sanctuary, not more enemies. This fool right here.

After Erice sheaths his sword and laughs, I jump and slap him upside the head. At least he has the decency to look sheepish.

"Keep your personality in check Erice." I shoot him daggers with my eyes. "Thank you for sanctuary guys, we'll be keeping to ourselves and out of trouble." I grab Erice's hand and drag him into the town before he can do something else to cause everyone to hate us before we even introduce ourselves, well, before I get to introduce myself.

The makeshift wall is made out of broken parts of something and stands a good seven feet tall or so. Some things look metal; some things I can't recognize. I swear what I thought were spears poking up from the ground is actual gigantic rib bones. What creature is that big? But I don't allow myself to stop and stare because I want to make sure we get inside before they decide to kick us out.

So far, I've only come across about twenty or so men here. Males. Where are the women? Every guy I come across is staring at me with a different look on their face, every man with a different face in general. I start to pull Erice by my side so he can protect me if anything happens.

When a one-eyed male who looks like he could use a sandwich reaches his arm out from my right in an attempt to touch me, Erice lunges right into his face and growls like a feral beast. Woah, I've never seen him like this.

"She's mine." He smiles his shark teeth at the male but the menacing aura coming off him is off the charts. It almost reminds me of Ruspin.

"I just wanted to see if she was real. She doesn't look like the other females dropped into the wastelands by the Underlord. Why would he let a female like this go?"

"He didn't let me go. He never had me." All the curious mumbles that were surrounding us like the buzz of bees stop. The sound of every male here turning to look at us is eerie, like trained zombies made to about-face at the exact same time. Each face looking at us is a creature from nightmares. No person is the same kind. Some with tails, some with multiple arms, missing noses, missing eyes, single eyes, tentacles, you name it. The one thing they all have in common is looking like they could use some more food and the cast of their skin tone. There's something sallow about it, something depressing and dark. Like this place leaves a cancer of darkness in them that will probably consume them over time.

"How can this be?"

"That doesn't make any sense."

"Where did you find her, Erice?"

"More like where did he steal her, Erice never just finds anything."

"Are there more like her out there?"

"Are you willing to share? I have things I can trade!"

"I have better things than he does, trade with me!"

My eyes start to widen more and more as the voices try to talk over each other rapidly, mostly shooting their conversation towards Erice like I'm not standing right here listening to them talk about me that way.

"How does she taste?" *No, he didn't.*

"HELL FUCKING NO. FULL STOP, RIGHT THERE." I'm not one to yell, but these guys right here need to be told. I bend my arms at my elbows and hold both my hands up, palms out. Might as well address them all, in case that statement inspires the other males' curiosity about how I taste. I'm sending every guy here daggers with my eyes. I might be the smallest one here, but...*hell no*.

Erice just laughs his booming laugh like the question wasn't ludicrous! I'm pissed at this fucker next to me right now and I pull a move I've seen him do. I crouch a bit and sweep my foot right at his ankles with all my might, making him fall on his ass.

The crowd is silent again, those with eyes blinking rapidly back and forth between Erice and me right before the buzz and roaring of voices start again.

"How do I get one of those!"

"Shit, I think I just came in my pants."

"Does she have a sister?"

"Does she want more men?"

"Female, I will trade for an hour with you!"

"I have better things to trade!"

"I offer you my sexual services for free!"

The sound of grunts and flesh hitting flesh can be heard. Some of these guys are getting rowdy, trying to get my attention by beating the other guys before they can shout their offers. This is getting to be insane.

At least we're getting a 'warm welcome' and not pitchforks I guess. It's the little things.

I leave Erice chuckling on the ground, trying to find a place that doesn't look claimed by makeshift tents or items on the ground so we can camp for the rest of the day and rest. All this testosterone is tiring me out physically and mentally. Erice's voice can be heard over the crowd arguing.

"That's exactly why she's my female. Keep your cocks

under control, gentleman. All she needs is Erice. I'm plenty." Now he's talking about himself in the third person. I can't.

I roll my eyes even if he can't see me do it. I'm going to lose all my brain cells the longer I hang out with Erice. I just know it.

CHAPTER NINETEEN

ERICE

My inserex is slicking up from the show of prowess my female just demonstrated in front of the guys. That fire in her always gets me hot.

Now I just need to keep them in line in case they think to steal her from me. I worked too hard to get her back.

Jumping back to my feet, I quickly rush to her side. Looks like my female wants to nest somewhere. Smart, we should. It's been a journey.

I've been in this camp every so often, so I know the layout and who usually sleeps where. Half the guys are missing, they must be on some sort of mission or hunting.

"Rest easy, little bit. I know just where we can camp. There is an unclaimed spot close to the outer parameter of this camp." I snatch up a blanket from someone's spot on my way over to my female. I'm sure the guy wouldn't mind making a good impression.

Straightening the blanket out on the floor when I reach

her, I pat the ground for her to relax. Sometimes she listens so well. That gets me hot too. She's perfect for me.

"Precious, I'm going to go out and see what the other guys are doing. To make sure food will be on the way for you." I grab one of my swords from my scabbard and offer it to her. She is small, but she is fierce, this I'm sure of. I see it in her eyes.

"Keep this while I'm gone. These men are good, but they can get...hungry when there is temptation in front of them." I offer her a smile to ease any of her fears, but she just curls her lip at me and grabs the sword. She is a cute little thing, isn't she? I chuckle at her antics.

"Watch out for the Ladir, he can never keep his hands to himself."

"How am I supposed to know who Ladir is?"

"He's the one with the multiple slimy limbs. You can't miss him." With a smile and a quick stolen kiss, I jump back before her swing hits my face in a loving touch and I'm off, jumping over the makeshift parameter wall. I can hear her lovely little fierce growl from the other side.

I know he's been following us; he's been doing it since the river. Does it make me a bastard for lying to my precious female? Probably, but it had to be done.

"Knight, you might as well show yourself. I'm not even sure how you were able to hide your presence this long with an ass like that." The sound of soft hooves comes out from behind the small, scattered gathering of trees that surrounds the back parameter of the camp, a few yards back.

"You're looking well. Last I saw, you were a little worse for wear limping away as the commander distracted me."

"Where is Kinsey?" Oh, look at him looking fierce. Well, not so fierce since he's weaponless and without his armor.

"I'm keeping her happy, if that is your true question."

"You have no right to her after what you did."

"Oh? I was just biding my time until I could retrieve her. She understands completely. In fact, I can still taste her thank you on my tongue."

I see the knight's leg shift before he even lunges. I decide to keep my sword sheathed to keep this an even battle. Don't want to take him down too quickly, where's the fun in that?

The sound of his hooves hitting the ground and the flesh-on-flesh impact of our fists probably echo to the camp, but no matter. I'll take care of this once and for all. This will be the last time little bit will mention this male's name. It should only be my name on her tongue and in her moans.

When he rears up his front legs, I roll onto the ground and away from his point of impact. Smart horsey he is, it was a trick of foot as he doesn't rear up all the way and instead back kicks me.

Thump.

I groan from the point of impact. My gut is going to feel this tomorrow. I'll just have to make Kinsey sit on my face instead.

Voices can be heard in the distance, and I bring myself back up to standing. I need to get this over with quickly before Kinsey finds out what I'm doing. She won't be happy finding me playing with her show pony.

Maybe she'll take her punishment out on me in delicious ways. I do like the thought of that as I continue to fight this male. Alright, I need to keep my head in the game. Thoughts of little bit are keeping me distracted.

I pull out my sword and take a swing, only to face precious right in front of Isra with my sword in her hand. My inserex is quivery and getting wet just looking at her like this.

Lowering my sword, I give Kinsey a smile. "Precious, you're going to have to step away. I'll finish up soon and come back to you the moment I'm done here."

"Shut up Erice. You're not finishing anything. In fact, I might just leave your ass right here and go off with Isra. How does that sound?"

I place my empty hand over my chest. "You wound me, little bit."

She lets out her cute little groan as she turns to Isra, rejected knight of the Underlord. What does she see in him besides being a show pony, hey? I can offer her so much more.

"Isra, where have you been?!" His face is still glaring at me, so I blow him a kiss. Seems he's not fully in her good graces just yet.

"I required extensive healing. I was of no use to you in the state I was in. But I followed you since the river, making sure this wasteland rat wasn't hurting you. I would have cut off his head for you if he did."

Sure. He's probably secretly a voyeur. I mean, I can work with that. I'll give him all the shows he wants while Kinsey rides my face. My mouth is watering at the thought of her taste.

"Isra, we've found sanctuary here. Why don't you join us? You shouldn't be out there alone." She is too precious, with too much heart for her own good. This will get her killed in the wastelands.

"You know what they say, little bit. Three's company and all that. Plus, you'll be too busy with me to bother with this reject, anyway."

"Erice, please shut up." Spicy.

Maybe I will keep the pony around just to rile her up. I should castrate him first, though.

"Kinsey. I'm not sure if the men here would welcome me. They know who I am."

"And I'm sure they know why you're out here without your armor. We'll stick together. Come on." My heart constricts with something that resembles heartburn and bile when I see her grab his hand and pull him after her. Maybe I should cut off his arms after I castrate him. This sounds like a good plan.

CHAPTER TWENTY

KINSEY

I can't believe Isra's here.

I *can* believe that Erice lied to me and does this kind of shit behind my back. I swear I don't know whether I should just abandon the bastard right here or stay for the protection this camp might offer. Knowing him, he'll probably just pop into my life again right when I least expect it.

The two sentries at the front entrance are watching my every move. When they see Isra behind me, they stand up straighter, both of them moving their hands over their weapons at the ready.

"Gentleman, he's with me. It's okay. He's part of my group."

"A knight of the Underlord this far out? He was sent to spy on us." The guy with the smile pulls out both his axes with this statement, legs bent and ready for battle.

Isra releases my hand and looks like he's ready for battle,

too. Anteater guy grins, it's the funniest looking thing, and pulls out both of his spears.

"Ah, the welcome party. Have at him men, I will be taking my female inside for some needed rest and relaxation." I literally turn and take a swing with my sword at this fucker right here. I can't stand him sometimes.

He jumps back and in a swift move, removes the sword from my hand and places an unwanted kiss on my mouth. I growl in frustration, thinking of all the ways I'm going to kill him in his sleep.

"Don't be like that, Kinsey. You know I strive to keep you happy and satisfied. The pony can stay with us until you tire of him." That wicked gleam in his now menacing smile is telling me he has plans for Isra. I need to keep an eye on him.

Isra is quiet. I wonder what he's thinking or planning.

"The commander and his troops are nearby. They lost our trail a few miles back. I made sure to create extra tracks to lead them astray. You can thank me by allowing me inside. We need to prepare for their impending arrival. If what I hear about the rebellion is true, then we need to make plans for action now."

The two sentries look at each other and the atmosphere changes dramatically, just like that.

"Half our men are out scouting or hunting. When the group returns, we will inform them of this. Plans of action will be made. It is time to finally take down the tyrant lord."

What did I step into? This sounds like a suicide mission. If half their men are out, that still makes only about forty. Can forty take down the castle? Who knows what other horrors lie inside?

I keep my mouth shut because I need to know the facts

before I make any assumptions. I just wanted to go home, not get involved in a rebellion.

The sentries step aside, allowing us entry back inside. When the males inside land their sights on Isra, some start drawing weapons while continuing to keep their distance, unsure of what's going on.

We continue a slow walk towards the sleeping spot Erice and I chose. I need to do something about these two. I have a feeling they're both going to kill each other in their sleep while I'm trying to kill Erice in his sleep.

What a trio we make. If you can even call us a trio at all.

"He's not sleeping next to you, precious. That pleasure is all mine."

"I wouldn't trust her with you with a long spear."

"You guys both need to shut up or I'm going to be sleeping alone and you guys can cuddle each other."

That shut them up just like I intended. But their eyes tell me their dick-swinging contest isn't over. Well...Erice is just a whole other breed of male. I guess I can't use that metaphor.

"Erice, who can I ask for some different clothes? This one is getting threadbare."

"You don't need any clothes, little bit, you have me. I can keep you covered."

"You are despicable."

"She loves me anyway."

"Miss! I heard you have need of extra coverings! I have plenty to trade!" The voice booms from somewhere behind me and I turn and see the antler guy from the front entrance.

"If you're here, who's out there?" One guy can't handle the front alone, can they?

"The other men have returned, and my shift has ended. I figured I'd properly introduce myself to the prettiest thing here."

"You've already met me, Drosk." Even though they both don't have eyes, I can tell they're glaring at each other. I must be going insane to even know that. What is this crazy place doing to me?

"That's very kind of you. What were you expecting to... trade for?" Do I dare ask?

Drosk opens his mouth, but the growl that comes out of Isra makes him open and close his mouth a few times before he finally decides on what he wants to say.

"I only ask that you grace me with your friendship." Oh, he's a smooth one.

I give him an honest smile and nod my head. He had one of his hands behind his back and is now bringing it forward. There is a folded khaki-colored item in his hand. I walk forward to take it as graciously as I can. Instead of making it simple though, the bastard grips my hand with the cloth still in it and gives a quick, chaste kiss on the back of it.

Slick.

Erice kills the moment by slapping Drosk upside the back of the head and I stifle a laugh because it's like watching dumb and dumber, truly.

Isra forces Drosk's hand open with his, causing him to emit a grunt of pain and hands me the fabric.

"Thank you, Drosk, I really appreciate it. Since you're here, where can I find some weapons?" A few of the males around us look our way again.

Somewhere further away I hear a groan and a mumble of, "I just came in my pants again."

"You can never control your cock anyway, that thing leaks all over the place."

"Get away from me, you disgusting creature."

"Come on, don't tell me she doesn't get your juices flowing."

Lord, save me from all these guys who have blue balls around me. That makes me think of Erice again, and his sackless crotch. Ugh, I need to stop thinking about him.

Drosk is still standing here. What is he waiting for?

"Um, thank you again Drosk." I nervously laugh and turn to kind of step behind Isra. I don't know what he's waiting for. Why isn't he going? Why does he still have that crazy smile on his face?

"Come now, the lady is tired. Thank you, friend, you can return to whatever rock you crawled from. Rest up, rebellion is coming."

"It looks like the other men have returned with meat." Isra's height gives him an advantage in seeing further up the camp. I am kind of hungry now that he's mentioned it.

As the boys continue to talk about whatever they're talking about, I unfold the cloth to find something that looks like a poncho. This will have to do, I guess. Maybe if I put a belt around it, it won't be so bad? The fabric is thicker than the dress I'm wearing and longer.

"Does anyone have a belt I can have?" I didn't think I was speaking that loudly when I hear some guys nearby scrambling and startling me. Some thuds ensue and groans. When I turn around, I see a couple of guys on the ground rubbing their heads in random locations and another male before me ripping the belt right off his own pants.

The moment he hands me his belt is the moment his

pants fall down to his ankles. *Dear lord.* His cock has three extra thin tentacles protruding out, and the base is extra thick with bumps all over it, like a blind woman's wet dream. There's probably a secret message encoded around his shaft. The head of his cock looks angular instead of a smooth mushroom and the longer I stare at it, the more it starts to rise, wanting to stare right back at me with its one eye.

I gulp, grab the belt swiftly and mumble a thank you before turning to hide myself behind Isra's farthest flank to simmer in my embarrassment and flaming cheeks away from prying eyes.

"The lady thanks you for your contribution. I ask that you leave our spot so she can get some rest, male." Isra doesn't sound thankful at all when there's a snarl at the end of the sentence. It gets the job done because the males near us scatter back to wherever their sleeping spot was.

The hustle and bustle of the other men returning with food distracts everyone enough to give us a semblance of privacy. Still holding onto my new items, I bend down to grab the blanket on the ground and move our spot a little farther away from everyone. There's way too much testosterone around me. I'm getting a little nervous.

Both Isra and Erice follow me and let me find whatever spot that makes me happy. The sun is probably going to go down soon and the sound of a roaring flame floats in the air, bringing the comforting smell of a campfire. Right when I'm about to sit down on the blanket, Erice drops himself onto his back with his hands behind his head. If he had eyes and eyebrows, he'd probably be moving them up and down by now. I stare at him in disdain and he just smiles at me, while bringing one of his hands out to pat his chest like he wants to serve as a living pillow for me. No. Give this fool an inch, and he'll take it all.

Isra makes to stomp on him with one of his hooves, and Erice rolls away, laughing. I scowl at his retreating back.

"Thank you, Isra." I rub his side before I sit down on the blanket. Isra soon lowers himself beside me, letting me use him as a backrest.

"So where do we go from here?" I ask either of the boys, hoping for an answer that calms the storm inside my mind over this potential rebellion.

"At this moment, we shall feast and rest until solid plans are made. Weapons will be required. I do not know how far the commander has come, if he's close or if he chose to go back for more reinforcements. It seems to me, with the Underlord's choice of sending out his best commander to find you, is that he will not rest until you are his. We need to keep vigilant at all times."

Isra's speech sounds so foreboding. His deep timber sending low-frequency vibrations against my back. I turn sideways to throw one of my arms over his horse body and rub my cheek against his fur for some comfort. I'm glad Isra is on our side, he'll have more information on the ins and outs of the Underlord's keep. This would give our little band of merry men an advantage, right?

As my eyes roam all the males in the sanctuary, doubts start creeping into my mind. How can this misfit crew of castoffs who look like they've seen better days take over the Underlord's keep? At the same time, what do I know? I'm not part of this world, really.

The smell of barbequed meat floats into my olfactory

senses, making my mouth water. When was the last time we ate? It always feels like we're on the go all the time.

"Come on, little bit. We should head to the front of the line before it gets too long." I take Erice's offered hand and get to my feet. As we walk towards the food, the small gathering crowd part like the red sea. This is beyond awkward because I know they're not parting for a menace like Erice. I can hear Isra's hooves softly walking behind us.

A sea of new faces I don't recognize stares back at me intently, then looks over my head to stare at Isra.

"So, the rumors are true then, an untainted female among our midst."

This statement comes from a creature I can't even wrap my mind around. He's spindly, looking like something mummified and wasted away. His head hangs low, much lower than his shoulder height, making him look like a hunchback even though he's not. His eyes glow and his parched and dry looking mouth looks like a ventriloquist when they're talking through their puppets; his lips barely move. His fingers are way longer than proportionate, and his bipedal legs bend backward. I swear it looks like he has no muscles. I don't know how they're holding him up. I can actually see through his forearm bones, like *see through* to the other damn side because there's not actually skin there. I can't tell if he has a nose or not because his head is wrapped in ripped strips of linen, reminiscent of the old world bandages, like a damn mummy.

"Yes, Bonard. The rumors are true. I sure do hope the rumors also state that the female is mine." Erice always has to metaphorically pee everywhere all the time. I'm tired of his shit.

"The Underlord wants her for his own. He has sent his top commander to retrieve her. The rebellion needs to start now before his troops can discover the whereabouts of this sanctuary and annihilate us before we can even start." Isra steps up in front of me to hide me from Bonard's sights.

"So the other rumors are also true, a banished knight amongst our midst. How very curious that these two things happen at once. What are the odds?" I can't tell if he's sarcastic, smiling, or what. His face doesn't change, and that makes everything all the more creepy.

"We're here to lend a hand in the rebellion, that's all that matters, Bonard. The more the merrier and all that." Everything is so simple to Erice.

Maybe I should learn from him and keep life simple too.

CHAPTER TWENTY-ONE

KINSEY

After our strange introduction to the other half of the rebellion, everyone ate and got along pretty well. I mean, no one died from any of the brawls that broke out.

The sun has gone down and I'm lying on the blanket, thinking over everything I've gone through up until this point. I still don't know how I got here. What happens after the rebellion is done? How do I get home?

I must have dozed off because I sometimes catch my eyes fluttering open when a shadow goes by. The sounds of everyone hunkering down in their own spots start to sound like another low hum buzz, lulling me into darkness. Whoever laid down beside me, wrapping their warmth around me, isn't helping either.

"You're mine. I can do whatever the hell I want with you and you can't do a damn thing about it."

"No!"

The fist that lands in my face causes pain to explode and stars to form in front of my eyes. There was so much momentum in the swing that it twisted my body and threw me on the floor, face down. There's something warm trickling and dripping from my nose. I'm not sure if it's the snot from my tears or if it's blood.

Before I can even think about it any further, my shorts and panties are ripped down my legs, hard. The burn from the friction makes me want to kick out, but he must have anticipated it because he grabs my legs before it can make a good kick.

My legs are manhandled through the struggles and sure enough, once my legs are free from any sort of protection from the clothing, my legs are forced apart and he comes up behind me. The sound of the zipper and belt buckle jingling will forever haunt my mind. When the warmth of his cock slides between my legs, poking and prodding, trying to reach my entrance, I give one final good struggle.

Who am I kidding? He has too much weight on me. I won't be able to escape. The silent tears continue to fall onto the floorboards beneath me as he shoves his hard cock into my dry pussy without invitation. The burn of the scrape branding me in my very soul.

Waylon got sent out again. I'm helpless to fight him off alone. I swallow down the pain, drown it out, dull it out with my mind as my thoughts take me away...

"Kinsey. KINSEY!"

I'm struggling, I'm fighting. I need to get away. I hate feeling so damn helpless! When a scream starts to tear out from my lungs, a large, warm hand clamps over it while someone whispers behind my ear.

"Shhh. Shhhh. It's me. It's me. I got you."

"Kinsey! Get the fuck off her!"

The cock is roughly pulled out of me, causing another scrape upon the exit, and I fall flat on the floor, my face buried in my arms as I continue to cry through the pain.

"Get out of my house, boy. You have no business here. If I catch you in my house again, I will cut you limb from limb and spread it out over the city so your mother will never find you." The menace in his voice is dripping with venom and I feel it as if it wants to seep into my very pores despite it not being pointed at me.

The sounds of grunts and flesh on flesh make me turn to see my father beating David until the blood is splattered all over his face, making him almost unrecognizable.

He drags his unconscious body towards the back door and once I hear the door open, the sound of a thud on the ground tells me he tossed him out like yesterday's trash.

I'm suffocating. I'm struggling. Get me out of this house! Get these arms off me! The sounds of flesh-on-flesh float to my ears again, and I'm trembling. I thought he was done. Stop the madness!

Sharp pain. The pinch inside my arm. It's become so routine it's almost a comfort. But the hands! The hands are holding me down! Why am I always held down?! Get away from me!

My father's menacing face comes back into view once the tears fall, clearing the blur. His face is splattered in David's blood as he climbs on top of me to finish what he started.

Someone's caressing my cheek, but I shake my head to get them off me. Stop! My soul can only take so much! I can't! Not when it's so damn clear. I need to float away.

"I'm with you." Someone's forehead is tenderly rubbing against mine, but I'm too scared to open my eyes. I'm sobbing silently despite the hand having been removed from my mouth. I can feel my lips trembling. I'm trying so hard to control it. Keep the weakness at bay. I don't want him to see it. My eyelids are my only shield. I don't want to see the dark depths of his depraved soul staring back at me, looking at me like his darkness wants to invade my senses and make me just like him.

A soft caress in my hair, a soft warm tongue slowly glides along my mouth, making me gasp for breath. It's too loving, it's not true. How can a broken girl like me deserve anything this soft? I'm too battered, too bruised, too battle worn.

When the tongue slips into my mouth in a slow stroke, my mind goes on autopilot and responds in the same cadence. It's tentative, it's careful, it makes me want to cry for different reasons.

"I will lay down my life for you to battle your demons, Kinsey. Use me, make me your anchor. Let me be your shield. Come back to me." How can he say such things? I'm not worth it. I've been crushed and pressed down for so long; I feel like I've lost myself in the darkness.

His tongue starts to dance with mine. I'm lost in his passion to bring me back from the brink. I find that I crave it. Perhaps I do need an anchor to keep me grounded and prevent me from washing away in this sea of darkness.

His kisses become hungry and demanding. I'm slowly being pulled back. He's the life preserver that wouldn't let me go. My fears are being stripped away a layer at a time as I open my eyes to find blood-red ones looking back at me. I can't tell if he's smiling, but I can feel his pride through his kiss. My eyes burn with the unshed tears. How can he want me so? Who am I but a battered and damaged soul? But the spark of hope I see in his blood-red gaze gives me a thread I hold on to. *Am I really worth saving?*

My hands cradle his face and pull him closer to me, as close as we can get. I want to drown out my senses and be consumed by the feelings he's invoking in me. *Breathe life into me, tell me I'm worth it. Tell me I'm worth saving.*

His kisses leave my mouth and travel down my neck to the top of my breasts. I must have been dreaming. We're still laying sideways facing each other on the blanket. When his hot mouth covers my nipple over my dress, my back bows to make him take more of me. I'm hot all over, my skin itches and strains to be free. This dress is too much. I'm tired of being constricted. Pushing him by the shoulders, he lifts his head in confusion and apprehension. When I remove my dress and toss it aside, he groans and pulls my body back towards his, his mouth covering my other breast. His nips and teases drive me higher. I can feel my body moving, asking for something so much more.

It's still dark out and the glowing embers that radiate from the campfire cause Isra's body to shroud me in darkness from potential prying eyes in his shadows. The sounds of snores around us cover the sounds escaping us in our explorations of each other's bodies. The hot and heady mixture of almost getting caught in the act in public.

Isra turns me to my stomach, and I let him. His hand brushes my hair to the side as his kisses trail from my neck to the end of my spine. I hear the rustle of his repositioning and suddenly his front hooves enter my line of sight as he lowers his back end behind me, doing his best to align our hips for the impossible, the connection of our bodies' anatomy. I raise my ass into the air in anticipation, feeling the underbelly of his body against my back. *Am I really doing this?* The tail end of my dream comes back to me, and I make the decision that I am. I need to get rid of these memories before they haunt me in my waking state, as well. A ghost that follows me around, hanging on my back like a demon waiting to devour.

If the demon is on my back, then I'll take Isra up on his offer and let him be my shield to these dark thoughts. I can feel the slide of his long cock against the lips of my pussy, it's hot and heady. He's rubbing it back and forth, teasing my clit. The fact that his cock can reach this far in his position tells me just how long he is. A small fear creeps up my spine, but maybe this is what I need. Maybe a new fear needs to chase the old ones out.

I know Isra wouldn't hurt me. He hasn't since the moment our paths crossed. This fact is what solidifies my decision right here, right now.

"Isra, I need you inside me."

He growls and starts to grind into me harder, across my lips and clit, creating sparks of pleasure, making me pant like a wanton pussycat in heat. When he pulls back and starts to prod at my entrance with just his head, I moan at the size of him. He's going to wreck me in the best ways, I just know it.

Each pull back and thrust gets him deeper and deeper, inch by slow inch. I'm panting even louder now, my pussy starting to stretch to accommodate what I want to take. The stretch almost becomes unbearable, the thin line between pleasure and pain. I can hear the wetness of my lips helping him slide in and out of me, it's the most erotic thing to my ears. That and his groans and snarls as he tries to hold himself back from pounding into me like he wants to.

A whine escapes my lips without intending to. It still feels like such a tease, this tempo he's taking. Is he purposely driving me mad? I need something raw, something more animalistic and primal.

I hiss under my breath, so as not to wake up the other males around us. "Fuck me Isra, stop teasing me!"

With a growl I haven't heard come out of him before, he rams his cock into me as far as he can go. I grunt from the enormous intrusion, filling me up to the brim and knowing that it's not all of him inside me makes me even wetter. He's so big, so long.

His front hooves are almost pawing and digging into the blanket and ground in front of me with his exertion. I feel like each thrust is pushing my entire body forward, so I try to push myself back at the same time to counteract the movement.

Each time he shoves it into me, I moan from the stretch and claw the blanket just like he is. The fine line between pain and pleasure is starting to blur the wetter and wetter I get. I need more.

Something this intrusive and big shouldn't feel this good, should it? It all feels so surreal right now.

"Isra, please." I don't even know what I'm begging for, but he starts to increase his pace and ferocity. I can hear him hold in another growl as his cock expands and the warmth of his release fills me up and spills out between his cock and my pussy lips. There's so much, we're still slipping and sliding against each other as his thrusts start to slow down until he shrinks enough to slip out of me. The smell of our combined juices and sex surrounds us, keeping us in a haze of lust. Well, me anyway.

My body relaxes onto the ground as Isra lands beside me on his side, panting like he just went through a horse race.

"I'm overflowing from just watching his cum squeeze out of you, little bit." Ugh, this perverted bastard. Isra seems to be in a post-orgasmic daze because he doesn't even bother to look or respond.

A warm body starts climbing over me from behind, slowly crawling up my legs. Erice pushes one of my legs to the side to open me up as his long, black tongue starts to lap at the juices coming out of me. He's so fucking dirty. Just like Erice to come in for this.

He groans into my pussy, sending vibrations along my lower lips, making me squirm.

"Oh precious, he didn't finish you, did he? That's what Erice is for. The pleasure is all mine." That shouldn't sound so hot. It shouldn't make my pussy clench so.

I let him turn me onto my back as he pushes both of my legs towards my shoulder. Without any hesitation, his face dives into my hot core with his tongue I love to hate and hate to love.

He plays my body like a pro, his tongue probing inside and around my clit until that spark from before climbs high like flames waiting to engulf both of us. My hand goes behind his head as my hips thrust with abandon against his face, telling him I want more.

He gives me just what I want and starts to do things I didn't know a tongue can do. When my pussy starts to clench and pulsate, my legs wrap around his head and he growls against my clit, sending me over the highest edge I've ever crested. I cry out in pleasure. I can't help it, moaning and writhing and whimpering as the climax dies down.

Moans and grunts from around the other areas nearby

can be heard like a chorus of orgies that rode the high with me. It's so empowering.

My legs fall to the side once the climax ends, and Erice climbs up to my face and forces his tongue into my mouth the way he always does. Always taking what isn't his. A shameless thief. But at this very moment, it's just what I need. Someone to selflessly give and then take something I wanted to give anyway, with a little resistance.

My arms wrap around his shoulders as my hands caress his bald head while our tongues tangle, giving me a taste of everything that's happened this night.

I should be ashamed. I shouldn't want all this. But the time has come for me to stop beating myself down just because my father isn't here to do it for me. The self-punishment has to end in order for me to let go of the darkness that tries to drown me in undeserved fear and misery.

CHAPTER

TWENTY-TWO

KINSEY

The morning's light makes me groan in irritation. I'm too tired. Just five more minutes. I turn my body and bury my face into the warmth of another person who's right by me. My arms automatically go around their neck to stave off the brightness of the orange sun.

This person smells of musk, male and earth. They also smell of cocky bastard as his hands start to take liberties and caress my naked ass, the fingers slightly grazing my pussy lips. Ugh! It's way too early for this shit. Without opening my eyes, I shove his shoulders away and turn my body around. The next body I snuggle up to is warm, his arms enveloping me in a chaste embrace, his face nuzzling against my neck. Ahh...this is so much better. He also smells of musk, male, and something else I can't put my finger on. I scoot myself closer to this warm body and start snuggling right back, nipping at his shoulder while I start to bring my body higher up so I can reach his mouth for a wet and not-so-chaste kiss.

He doesn't disappoint as he groans into my mouth, making me writhe and rub myself against his body as if to mark him with myself.

"Do you have need of my services, my dark queen? My cock is happily at your disposal." *Oh my.*

I moan into his mouth and continue to duel with his tongue in a battle for dominance, all the while with my eyes still closed.

A throat rudely clears behind us, and I'm pulled off my knight abruptly.

"We have a full day ahead of us, little bit. Let's leave the horny pony to his own needs while we ready ourselves for the rebellion." What a cockblocker.

With an exasperated groan, I open my eyes and glare at Erice, who currently has a smirk on his face.

Sitting up, I stretch my body before I realize that I'm butt fucking naked. I quickly cross my arms over my chest and private areas while Isra takes the opportunity to stand himself up to provide me with some sort of shield from prying eyes.

Some groans can be heard nearby, but I ignore them as I quickly gather my new fabric and belt, throwing it over myself to make a makeshift dress. Yes, this will do, it's a much thicker fabric. I lift my arms to make sure I have good movement, but it only serves to rub the fabric against my nipples, making them perk up. The fabric reminds me of burlap fabric, but what choice do I have? It covers me more than my thin cotton dress.

Speaking of, I don't want to lose my cotton dress. I don't know why, but something in my gut tells me I need to keep it with me. Wrapping it around my head and neck, I figured I could use it like a block to the sunlight.

We roll up the blanket to pile it to the side. The three of us walk over to the growing crowd in the middle of the camp.

Drosk catches us coming closer and raises his olive arm in greeting. That smile of his really is disturbing.

"Greetings! Come with me and we'll fit you with some weapons. It seems we will march out tonight to bring us closer to the keep. We are meeting another part of our rebellion, the males on the inside behind enemy lines."

Ah, now this makes more sense. Their little outfit here doesn't seem so hopeless now. Seems they have more help than I thought, on the inside at that.

Isra follows Drosk towards another group who are hovering around some weaponry. Erice's tail starts to travel up my leg, making me turn to scowl at him. He smiles, of course, like it's all a game to him.

The whole camp is moving back and forth, preparing for a march. I give Erice's tail a slap when the sound of Isra's hooves comes towards us. He's outfitted with some sparse and crude armor on his body, as well as strapped with a sword and what looks like a bat with spikes at the end of it.

Bonard is saying something, and the crowd starts to quiet down. Everyone turns to look at him.

"We head east until the halfway point. Our second group will be awaiting our arrival. Gear up men, we are getting closer to taking down the tyrant king. Don't let your guard down." The crowd roars with an agreement and the sounds of metal and movement can be heard all around us as everyone starts to exit the makeshift sanctuary.

We march across plain lands, and we march across multiple groupings of trees. I'm not even paying attention really, just following along with Isra and Erice by my side. Sometimes Drosk hangs out with us, but Erice doesn't like to be outshone. I don't know what he's jealous about since he's the one who always leaves me behind. Yeah, I'm still salty.

When we reach our destination, we make camp. The three of us chose to camp more towards the back of the group. I don't know who this other group is, not sure if I should trust them yet. Someone makes a campfire, and we all settle in.

I volunteer to find some branches and twigs to help with the fire, looking more towards the direction we came from since we cleared it already. I'm bending down to add a pretty good looking piece of branch to the batch in my arms when the hairs on the back of my neck stand up right before I feel a suffocating and dominating presence behind me. My heart is starting to race, and my nervousness is taking over my mind. I quickly tell myself I can use one of the bigger branches as a weapon. I drop my bundle on the floor and grab the biggest one I have right as I turn around to take a swing.

A solid hand grabs the branch before it even makes contact. I'm face to face with someone I didn't think I would see again so soon.

My breath leaves me like a whisper. "Ruspin?"

He yanks the branch that I'm holding onto, and it brings me closer to his body. He tilts his head and sniffs me along the crook of my neck, making goosebumps appear.

"You've seemed to have fared well since we've last spoken." His voice is gruff right by my ear, and it does something to me. It sends a strange feeling down my body. Before

I can try to decipher what that feeling is, he lets me go and twists to parry a blow from Isra.

Someone grabs me from behind and throws me over his shoulder, dislodging my head wrap. When his tail wraps around my wrist, I know exactly who it is. Erice deposits me back in the heart of the camp right before he leaves to do who knows what. Drosk runs over to me, checking me over.

"Are you alright? Where is Erice going?" My heart is still hammering. I don't know what's going on myself.

"T-the commander of the Underlord's army." Drosk visibly relaxs and I'm left questioning what the hell is going on.

The sounds of blades clashing and grunts flow into the air as a few of the males in the group gather to see what's amiss.

I'm too antsy sitting here, wondering if my guys are alright. I run towards the sound of fighting as well and stop abruptly when I see Erice groaning on his feet, wiping blood from his lips, and the commander with his boot on Isra's form on the ground with his arm blade at his neck.

"Commander. I see you've come to join us." The calm voice comes from behind me. I turn to see Bonard walking towards the scene. Does he know the commander? What does he mean 'come to join us'?

"Bonard, I see you're starting to pick up riffraff from the wastelands in your group." Bonard laughs, and it sounds like he's dying. It's croaking and sounds like he has phlegm lodged in there.

"What the hell is going on?" I need this fool to let my men go. "Ruspin, I'm going to need you to step away from my men."

His smile is feral in my mind as he takes his boot off Isra's form, his arm blade reshaping back to its original form. "Your *men*? I didn't know you were collecting." My heart is still beating wildly. Ruspin's presence is so oppressing and encompassing. It's everywhere, and it's commanding everyone around him for respect, to submit. The closer he gets to me, the more I feel like cowering away. But I can't.

"You know of our commander then, female? He is who we were meeting up with. He leads the rebellion from within the keep's walls."

What? I can't even concentrate on what Bonard is saying because the commander has locked on me with his gaze. It's penetrating and I'm afraid to look away, I'm afraid to submit that way. The way his muscles move like the ultimate predator just waiting for a chase.

I'm still caught in his trance when Erice steps in front of me, breaking the spell. An animalistic growl emits from him, and it makes me shiver with its ferocity. Or am I shivering for other reasons?

"It seems, you didn't get enough of me the last time we crossed paths, Rewsk." How can a voice spoken so low, sound so powerful?

"The female is mine." Oh, Erice. I don't think that's a good idea. The commander is a different breed of male.

"Step down, Rewsk. You need me more than this group needs you." Shit, he might be right. I place a calming hand on Erice's back.

Erice snarls but visibly relaxes his battle stance. Isra is behind the commander, panting, with his eyes glowing even redder than I've ever seen him. He looks like he's holding onto a thread too.

The commander just stares at me and side-steps towards Bonard, who stands behind me to the left.

"The plans remain the same. Your males will march from the back, while my troops set up from the inside." He casts his eyes towards me again for a short period. "I think I may have a way to distract the Underlord for our upheaval."

What? What does that have to do with me? Why is he looking at me like that?

When we make it back to the heart of the group, I see that the elven troops that follow Ruspin are already there intermingling with the other males. Have they been in on the rebellion this entire time? I couldn't even tell when they last held me hostage. I guess that's the point, to blend in.

Ruspin and Bonard go off to speak of tactics while my men and I return to our camp spot.

"That bastard just can't stay away. No worries, little bit, I won't let him get to you."

"You talk a big talk when it was the commander who almost cut your head off."

"It's the game we play, he and I." Erice brushes it off with a dismal wave of his hand.

"Kinsey." My head jerks to the side when my name is called by a voice I didn't think was going to talk to me again this day.

Ruspin is standing there a few feet away. I'm almost scared to answer. The boys are getting tense, but now that we know he's part of the rebellion, none of them are making a move just yet.

Ruspin isn't bothered at all by the boys' reaction. "May I have a word with you?"

I take a big gulp and pat both of my guys to let them

know I'll be okay before walking slowly towards Ruspin. *I hope I'll be okay.*

He doesn't wait for me to reach him but rather turns to lead me somewhere more private, I assume. I feel like I'm walking towards the guillotine.

We stop quite a way away from the group and from prying ears.

Ruspin corners me against a tree and leans in to sniff me again. What is up with him? Why is my heart pounding like this?

"Kinsey..."

I gulp and try to stay confident. "Yes, Ruspin?"

"You smell of males and it angers me. You should smell of me. How do you think I should fix this?" What? I thought he wanted to talk to me about the rebellion, not this.

His tongue travels along my jaw, his hot breath sending tingles down my spine. *Woah.* The cool and reserved commander. I thought he was going to chew me out about escaping his clutches or something. Anything but this.

"I think it best..." His tongue continues a slow discovery of my collarbone, "that I return you to the keep so as not to arouse suspicion with the Underlord." His hands suddenly appear on my hips as he brings his body even closer to me, pushing me against the tree's bark.

"We allow the Underlord to feel he has his prize, and while he's distracted by you..." His tongue is doing wicked things to my skin. It almost feels like he's writing notes along the surface of my skin. "... the troops will come in from the back." His hot breaths are so close to my mouth I'm almost salivating for it, though I shouldn't. "While my men will be dismantling the possibility of anything going awry from within." I'm panting as he speaks of his plans almost against my lips, dangling a possibility of something in front of me without the promise of actually giving it to me.

Erice and Isra are more than I can handle. The commander is too much for me. He overwhelms my senses. But he also excites something within me. The forbidden. I shouldn't like the male who wanted to turn me into the Underlord, right? But then again, wasn't Isra in that position not that long ago?

He presses in closer to me. I didn't think he could. When his mouth is just millimeters from mine, he stops. We're both panting at this point, both staring into each other's eyes.

"I promise you, I will come for you, Kinsey. You have my word. But you must see the plan through, endure until I get there." His mouth graces mine with every syllable he speaks. I shouldn't feel this way. Not with what he's proposing. He's going to turn me over to the Underlord and the rebellion will be brewing in the background until they can come to get me. But what will happen to me in the meantime?

"How can I trust that you will keep your word?" I feel a little vulnerable. Ever since I landed in this place, I've been helpless, always relying on the help of others to make it. But something in the commander's gaze is telling me that he wouldn't break his word. This little dance we're playing with how long we can just continue to speak against each other's mouths without actually planting them on each other is driving me mad.

"Trust me. A man of honor will always keep his word."

"How can I tell if you're a man of honor? Why *should* I trust you?"

"Because, dear Kinsey, I would have ravished you and

stolen you away by now. Instead, I let those fools think they have you while I hold myself back from what I'm really hungering to do."

My breath hitches and my next sentence comes out in the quietest of whispers. "What do you want to do to me?" Knowing might kill me. Not knowing might kill me, too.

"Many, many things, little female. Things that would make you cry for mercy and cry for more at the same time." I squeeze my thighs together as much as I can discreetly, but Ruspin knows.

My heart is pounding out of my chest, he's too much. I turn and run away from him like the coward I am, slipping past under the arm he had placed on either side of me against the tree trunk. Two males are enough. I can't. He's worse than Isra and Erice combined.

When I make it back to our camp spot, the boys look me over. Erice jumps to his feet and his hands are roaming me, searching for I don't know what. I stop his hands, grab his face, and give him a peck on the cheek to reassure him before stepping towards Isra and letting him hold me in a tight embrace.

Nothing more is said as we eat and settle in for the night. My mind is still running through what Ruspin proposed to me. Do I trust him? Do I hand myself over the Underlord who has been described as the tyrant king? What if he doesn't let me go? What if Ruspin doesn't make it to me in time?

CHAPTER TWENTY-THREE

KINSEY

When the group makes it to the edge of the last cluster of trees, we stop to stare at the dark sight before us.

The back of the castle is carved into the shape of a damn skull, with the exit point being a gaping mouth. The deep carving for the eye sockets looks like it can see into your very soul, unraveling all the plans you have against it. Some bat-like creatures fly out of the nostril opening, only adding to the creepy haunted house feel I'm getting from it.

Except it's not just a haunted house, it's a damn keep full of horrors. The memory of the Grapner comes back to me and I shiver. Am I really agreeing to this? Letting myself get caught by a king that everyone wants to kill? What will he do to me? This leads me back to one of my previous questions about this place...where are all the females?

"Kinsey, with me."

"Pray you keep your word commander, or it will be your head on the spit for our next feast." Isra is pissed about the plan, but he hasn't said much about it. Erice has been quiet and contemplative.

Ruspin doesn't even bother to answer Isra. He continues to look at me and raises a hand, palm up, waiting for me to accept my fate in this plan.

I owe these guys, don't I? So many of them have kept me alive up to this point. Ruspin promised me he'd come get me when it's time. What do I have to lose? I also still need to find my way back home. Once the issue with the king is taken care of, these guys can help me get back, I hope.

Slowly placing my palm on his, Ruspin grips my hand firmly and tugs me behind him towards his troops.

"Bonard, have your males rest up and wait for my signal. If not directly from me, then my second, Khez." Bonard brings his arm up in agreement as Ruspin continues to pull me along.

When we are out of earshot of the original group, Ruspin places me in front of him as we march around the keep to enter from the front. His troops follow right behind us without a word. I almost jump out of my skin when Ruspin places one of his hands on my hips.

"Say nothing of the rebellion, no matter the tricks the Underlord might pull. You must stay strong until the plan plays out. It's the only way this will work. If my countenance and words baffle you, you must play along." He mumbles these instructions behind me as we trudge along the path. I'm starting to get kind of scared. What is he implying? What's going to happen to me? My mind becomes distracted with the vision of the keep's garden coming up.

It doesn't look any better this time around. The mindless zombies who pace the front still look just as depressing as the first time.

When the troops walk the straight path towards the entrance, I hear the zing of swords slicing through the air and gurgles. Looking around quickly, some of the troops have chopped down some of the zombies that have wandered too close. Heads are rolling haphazardly, and limbs are littered in different locations. The other remaining walking dead are tripping over some of the dismembered limbs, getting entangled with their chains, causing a rattling sound to mix in with the sound of wet flesh continually hitting the ground. Couldn't these guys just kick them back or something? The ground darkens as it becomes bathed in blood, the smell of petrified flesh becoming stronger.

The doorway is just as massive and foreboding as I remember. It opens like a damn mouth of hell with jagged edges that remind me of teeth. I try to keep my breathing calm by breathing slowly in and out of my mouth. Once we pass the mouth, Ruspin leads me to the right. The hallway we find ourselves in has peeling wallpaper on the walls. The color is drab and reminiscent of days lost. Has this place ever looked brighter? Probably not. There are crooked images hung every now and again along the sides. Some of these images have been slashed through with something sharp, other images are covered in cobwebs, distorting the picture beneath it. Whatever the image is, it isn't human looking. The path becomes darker and darker the longer we walk. It's creeping me out when I can't see what's ahead.

I'm directed to take a left along one of the forks in the hallway. This hallway has a light of sorts at the end of it. The echoing sounds of the troops' footsteps create a beat in my chest.

When the hallway opens up, my eyes widen. It's a throne room from hell. What am I looking at? There's a creature dancing provocatively in front of the thing, sitting on the stone throne.

This creature has pink flesh that spans primarily from her head to her chest. There are no eyes, no nose, and voluptuous lips. A large black twisty horn protrudes from the top of her head and a smaller one from the back of her head.

But, oh my hands. There are hands everywhere. Four that come from her back, four from the front. Each is blacked and tipped with claws. They all writhe with her dance as she swings her body left and right, lost in the moment. Her bottom half is a group of black tentacles of various sizes, not one is sized the same. It glides with her movements, leaving a thickly coated slime everywhere she touches. When my eyes go back to her torso, you can see two small buds for her breasts and a large angry-looking scar that starts from the middle of her neck going straight down between her ribs until it disappears into the blackness of her legs.

The king, who I assume is sitting on the throne, looks bored out of his mind. I don't know how I can tell because there really isn't a face there either, not that I can see yet. He's utterly disgusting looking. His skin is wrinkled from having too much of it. His feet, which are lifted up onto the throne, are tipped in talons that are reminiscent of an eagle about to grab you and eat you alive. The skin on his head is folded forward like the end of an uncircumcised dick, while the top of his head sports a good handful of filaments that jut out. Extra layers of skin are folded over his pecs, but don't hide the wrinkly skin that covers his protruding ribs. His hands are tipped in claws as well, from what I can see as they hang over the armrest of the throne. He looks like he's sitting on an over-large cloak that covers the chair. But the longer I stare, the longer I realize this is skin too. What the hell? This particular skin is so large, it looks like it's melting onto the ground before the throne.

I don't know if I can do this. I don't know if I can stay with this Underlord long enough for Ruspin to come to get me. I take a step back, wanting to run out of here when I hit a warm body. Ruspin's hands grip my shoulder tightly as he addresses the king.

"We have retrieved the female, Lord." The female. That's me. I stand out like a sore thumb in this dark place. Movement from behind the throne catches my eye.

I take a large gulp and clamp my mouth so to stifle the scream that wants to come out. There is another female who walks out. She has no arms, her head and chest are smooth, her beautiful breasts moving with her walk. Her face looks like someone ate it, chewed it, and spit it back out while having a million nails hammered into it. It looks like fucking hamburger meat. Her torso ends where her rib cage ends. You can see her exposed spine in all its horrific glory as she walks around the king, swinging her hip bones. Her legs are long and beautiful like the top of it doesn't have missing organs. How is this possible? What is this place?

The Underlord hasn't responded and with the way the skin folds over his face, I can't tell if he's even looking at us.

If this is what females look like in his court, what is going to happen to me? I'm so scared, I think I feel myself shaking.

Ruspin's grip tightens on me, and I try to swallow the bile that wants to come up.

The voice that echoes into the room is deep and gravely. It makes me want to scratch my ears out. It makes me think of *death.*

"You've been a hard one to catch, female with the eyes of death. All who wander this kingdom belong to me. I'm glad the commander was able to complete his mission; unlike the knights I've sent out before. Worthless creatures they are. I'm glad I didn't have to dispose of my best commander as well." A strange insect-like sound comes from above us and when I lift my head to look. I do scream.

There is a creature that looks like a humanoid attached to the ceiling, but its head is on backward and his back has been peeled open and filleted. There is a bloody-looking mass of a tail that extends from his back, coming towards us. The end of the tail looks like it has nostrils, and I don't want to know if it has a mind of its own. What the hell is that thing?!

"Silence female! The noises that emit from your mouth are disturbing my pets. Perhaps I shall put that mouth of yours to better use. Leave us!"

Ruspin and the troops about-face and just leave me to my doom.

CHAPTER TWENTY-FOUR

RUSPIN

The ability to mask my emotions has kept me in position as commander of the Underlord's army. But that tight mask almost slipped when I heard Kinsey scream. I couldn't allow a small slip to ruin the plans we have. Taking my hands off Kinsey felt akin to cutting them off. But it had to be done. The king cannot know of what's to come. He sits there on his stone throne, playing his people like pets and puppets. My eyes see red just thinking of what the king has in store for the female. His quick dismissal of my men and I is just what I needed. I couldn't stand to smell Kinsey's fear anymore. I need to keep my mind on the task ahead.

The Underlord will be taken down, even if it means losing my own life in the process. His propensity for playing with all the females in the realm and disposing of the rest of his kingdom like they are trash will end. The world we live in has been on a slow decay since his ascent to the throne.

Things must be changed or else none of us will have a world left to live in.

My men have been briefed about the internal battle plans. We terminate and get rid of anyone who arouses suspicion and anyone who is suspicious of our tactics. Half the creatures left in this keep are mindless, but the other half are conniving and tricksters making you believe they know less than they do. The true task here is to determine which is which. A task that must be done quickly to pave the way for the other group to infiltrate.

The female must stay strong until the end comes near. I must stay strong enough to not kill the king myself, exposing us for what we are.

As we walk down the hallways, my men split in two. One group will distract the King's court, while the group that remains with me will continue on into our barracks, gathering supplies for the others outside. Hidden tunnels are found everywhere in this keep. Having been born here under the prior ruler, I relay the castle's underground map to the remaining men, making sure to remind Khez of the signal he must relay when the time is right.

Time is of the essence, and I pray the female is strong enough to withstand the Underlord's cravings.

CHAPTER TWENTY-FIVE

KINSEY

The female with her multiple hands made my skin crawl as the Underlord gave her the command to 'fit me' in my new wear, essentially stripping me bare before everyone here as I'm paraded like a new pet with just a collar and chain.

When the Underlord stepped from his throne, I came to find that the excess skin that spilled onto the ground was actually part of his back, a back that sports flesh wings. It's disturbing. It covers him like a damn cape, not like those cool gargoyle movies. As he walks, holding onto my chain and pulling me behind him, I'm stuck staring at his back and the way the wing skin still drags on the floor. The only thing that comes to my mind in comparison with the way his skin looks is foreskin. His entire body just looks like foreskin that's wrinkling and sagging in places. Though his build puts him a head taller than me, his bones sticking out make me wonder why the kingdom fears him. Is it just his authority? Or is there something else I'm not seeing yet?

I forget to look around and pay attention to my surroundings by the time the Underlord brings me to his bedroom. If you can call it that. There are cages, some on the floor, some hanging, all occupied with different creatures that look like they're on the verge of death. The bed in the middle of the room has torn and weathered red sheets on it. Why does it look that way? Are some parts of it singed?

He jerks my chain, and I fall to my knees. He turns to look down at me while I cough from the collar, choking me. When my eyes go up, I still can't see his face. His damn face and his damn folds of skin cover him in darkness.

"You are my most prized possession. You belong on your knees before me, just as you are, always." The fucker actually pets my head like I'm a pet. He's so disillusioned. If I wasn't so damn scared of what he would do to me, I'd tell it to him to his face right now. But I don't want to sabotage the plan before it can even get started. Ruspin told me I needed to hold on, to survive until he gets me. I'm going to try my best.

Right before my very eyes, what looks like overgrown folds on his crotch turns into a cock protruding out right into my face.

"Please me female and I'll let you sleep in the bed tonight." Shit, what other choice do I have? I'm chained like an animal at this bastard's disposal.

His clawed hands reach down and grasp his cock firmly. It starts to grow hard, rising up to attention as his hand peels back his extra skin to expose a head that is already sliming up with something.

"That's right. That's exactly where you should always be." I'm

crying silently but he doesn't care. He just continues to unzip his pants, pull out his cock to stroke it in front of my face in a slow rhythm.

"Open up, baby, take it all in. That's it. That's a good girl."

"Open up female and take it all in." I'm scared. I'm shaking my head and trying to pull myself back, but he just jerks the chain hard, bringing me forward. My face falls against his cock, the slime sliding against my cheek as he groans and continues to grip and tug.

"Refusing me will come with dire consequences, female, and I wish not to break you just yet. Your purity amplifies my desire. Just open up your mouth and make it easy on yourself for tonight. Though it excites me to know you may crave my punishments for I do so like to play with my toys."

Tears are falling down my cheeks. I'm fucking stuck. Do I just take it and hope it pacifies him for tonight, or do I fight? But what if it messes up our plans?

His other hand grasps my jaw painfully as his thumb invades my mouth, making me open up.

"That's it, little female. The warmth of your mouth makes me want to release my seed right here. Open up and take me in." He doesn't give me a choice because his hand slaps my face hard, ringing my ears as he forces his cock into my mouth in one thrust.

I'm choking, gagging, and when I inadvertently swallow, he groans. When his hips come back, my eyes catch something happening to his head. The skin that envelops and covers his face pulls back like a fucking cock, revealing what's underneath. I hate it. I fucking hate it because what's underneath is a handsome face that can rival the gods. His strong roman nose, the cleft on his chin, his angled cheekbones can't hide the serrated teeth that show when he smiles down at me at his mercy. His eyes are piercing, the color of a golden sunset. It roams all over my face as his lavender tongue pokes out to lick his luscious lips.

His hips continue its languid thrusts into my mouth, forcing me to take his length as I struggle to breathe through the act. My mouth is filling with saliva to ease his entry, spilling out the side of my mouth and dribbling down my chin. When he starts to move faster, I can see the skin over his bony body start to expand and contract from his breathing. His protruding hip bones are a sight for sore eyes. How can there be such a contrast to this creature? How can he look so beautiful as he hides behind folds and layers of evil?

He drives himself into me. I can feel his cock growing in my mouth, making my jaw ache. When the taste of something foul starts to fill my mouth, I gag and bite down. He groans, punches me in the face, and drives himself deeper into my mouth until it starts to fill up with his foul seed. It tastes disgusting and sour. It makes me want to gag.

He laughs as he pulls himself from my mouth and holds the top of my head and jaw together to clamp it shut, forcing me to swallow.

"That was naughty, little pet. I do love naughty things." He bends down until his face is in front of mine. "I think we'll have lots of fun together, you and I." He taps the side of my face like it's endearing before he bellows something I can't understand.

My head whirls back as the sound of nails on the hard floor comes closer to me. My fucking god, I should have never turned to see.

A creature on four limbs tipped with one giant claw each,

two extra limbs in the front, and 3 heads that are attached to three long and pocked marked necks stare at me. Each head has long black hair like mine, each head with eyes devoid of color. The front claws remind me of a spider, making my insides churn.

"You have become my most favorite toy yet." The Underlord's warm breath whispers against the back of my ear as I watch in horror when the new creature morphs in front of my eyes into what looks like a flesh cage. I'm caught by surprise since I'm still staring in shock as the Underlord kicks me inside and the creature locks me up between four geometric walls of fleshy bars. When I turn to look at him, the cage moves. Moves! I get higher and higher until I'm almost at head height with the Underlord.

"Come, I like to keep my pets close by in case I feel the need to play." The cage walks behind the Underlord as he exits his bedroom. The low moans of the other creatures in the cages in his room haunt my mind right before the bedroom door closes shut, silencing their voices.

CHAPTER TWENTY-SIX

ERICE

How long is this bastard supposed to take? Little bit is in the bowels of hell and I hate not knowing what I'm walking into. I should have killed the commander when I had the chance. But if I did that, our rebellion wouldn't have men on the inside. This has become more than just an inconvenience.

I'm eyeing the knight as the men out here speak of tactics and possible outcomes. He cares for my precious, I'll give him that. I allow her to keep him until she tires of him. Dammit, I should be with her. I should be shielding her from whatever nefarious plans the Underlord has for her. What need does he have of another female when he has collected all the females of this world to become a dying harem? Each time he 'graces' us with a discarded female, the creature is nothing but skin and bones on the verge of death, the soul already gone when you look them in the eyes.

I refuse to let precious become that. Become a thing to be used and discarded. She is mine. And I take care of what is mine. I don't trust the commander and his 'word'. What good is it if my precious comes out battered and broken to the soul to become a shell of herself?

Jumping down from the tree I've perched on, I quickly slide myself away from the group and start to look for other possible entrances into the keep.

"I'm coming for you Kinsey, hold on for me, little bit."

CHAPTER TWENTY-SEVEN

KINSEY

Sleep with one eye open around these parts, Kinsey girl. No one is to be trusted. Everyone is an enemy, especially the ones with a smile. They use your vulnerabilities to their advantage right before they shove their pills down your throat and tie you up to make you compliant.

"And I should trust you then?"

He smiles a cruel smile, leaning down to my height before lowering his voice. "No, you should never trust me."

I awake with a start, my heart pounding out of my chest. Where am I? What the hell?

I'm in a metal box, I think. It's small. I'm crouched and can't get into a good sitting position. My hands are roaming every surface I can touch, hoping for a latch for anything. A light turns on behind the metal, and it looks like a two-way plexiglass of sorts and not metal like I initially thought. But it's cold to the touch.

What I see on the other side makes my blood run cold.

Each surface is lined with spikes facing inwards. I don't know how far they are from the plexiglass but a hum and vibration starts. My heart is beating erratically as the spikes start moving towards me, closing in. I feel so closed in. I can't breathe. No. No. Someone stop the spikes. Please!

The sound of metal grating on metal makes the plexiglass vibrate even more and I swear I can feel it down to my marrows. I don't know what to do. The screeching... it's invading my mind; I can't think straight. The walls are closing in on me. What if this plexiglass is actually a figment of my imagination? What if the spikes can poke through it? I'm shaking as I curl into a ball into the fetal position, trying to make myself as small as I can.

I'm going to die. I'm going to die in a box of spikes. This is the end. I can't. Ruspin, Erice, Isra, where are you? I need to be saved. I always need to be saved. My face is getting wet from my tears and I'm too afraid to uncurl. Afraid to see the spikes right before it pierces me in the eyes. My mind is already imagining the liquid that squirts forth as my blood starts to get drained from the multiple holes that will pierce through my skin.

The room is stifling. Please! I'm shaking. I'm pissed. I'm afraid. I scream!

The hum stops, air enters the cell, I feel hands. Hands everywhere! Hands all over me! They're pulling me every which way. I'm still screaming, trying to scramble away, but I fall off the ledge and land on the ground. The walls must have disappeared, but I can't concentrate on that. I feel bound. I'm pulled, I'm pushed, someone is trying to rip my hair out.

When I open my eyes, I wish I didn't. There are heads

everywhere. Heads on spider crab legs. The eyes are clouded over and some of their mouths have been ripped open. I'm kicking and screaming. The creature pulling my hair looks like a child whose face has been torn vertically from his upper lip to its nose. Its bowels are spilling out, but the claws that tangle themselves in my hair are leaving sharp pains and scratches along my scalp.

The sound of something large and metal crashing into the ground makes all these little creatures of nightmares run away like roaches in the light. I'm sobbing onto the ground, still crouched. Where the fuck am I?

When the pain in my scalp subsides, I pick up my head and see the Underlord looking down at me. His hand shoots out and grabs my hair right before his flesh wings expand to their full size. I don't anticipate it, and it jerks my head almost off my neck when he shoots to the air with one beat of his wings.

My screams echo into the hallways as we fly from room to room. The wind is cutting my face, or are those hands reaching out from the walls?

I feel like I'm floating when I'm tossed into the air and land hard on a mattress with frayed and disheveled sheets. It's not the same room from the last time, no. This room houses something crawling on the ground. It looks like a torso that's been torn from its bottom half, the spine still leaving a trail of blood wherever it goes.

The Underlord grabs the creature by the neck and I see that it's a female with the shape and size of her breasts. Her eyes, my god, her eyes. They've been removed, and the wound is ripped and dirty, picking up all the dust that she's trailed across.

What the hell is this guy doing?

He walks to the bed, drops himself beside me onto his back as he brings the half torso up with him. It's fucking disgusting, disturbing, and sad.

His cock extrudes from his skin folds and the Underlord begins to force the female's face onto it, fucking it for all it's worth, all the while smiling at me with his handsome face. How can something so beautiful be so fucking evil? I can't take my eyes away from the other female as I watch in horror when he breaks her jaw on his final thrust, his seed leaking out the side of her mouth.

He tosses her body to the side with a wet thud as he continues to stroke his cock with her blood and semen mixed together.

"I'm going to savor you for last, little female. I'm going to torture myself and hold off until you become my final female."

Final female? What then? What the hell does he have planned for me? He must read my thoughts, because his next answer chills me.

"You will be the vessel that carries my heir. I will very much enjoy destroying your body from the inside out. Who knows, perhaps you will enjoy it too."

I turn my face and bury it in the sheets. I can hear his maniacal laughter next to me, as well as the sound of his hand angrily stroking his wet cock to another completion. His groan makes me want to choke on my tears.

I don't know how long I can handle this. My heart hurts for the female. How long will the rest of his females continue to live like this?

Guys, I need you. Please hurry!

CHAPTER

TWENTY-EIGHT

RUSPIN

The sound of Kinsey's screams grates my soul with fire. I can't stand it. My hands and blades itch to annihilate the king and bathe in his blood. My chest constricts at the thought of what Kinsey might be enduring in his little games of torture. She must stay strong. We are so close.

My troops have slowly started eliminating those who are loyal to the king. One by one they fall like the pawns they are. The initial steps in toppling the king are to weaken his foundation. A foundation built on lies and deceit. Every male beyond their first century knows of how the king toppled his prior predecessor.

The wails and screams of pain attracted the troops within the keep. Every foot soldier, including myself, rushes towards the throne room only to find the walls painted in crimson. What was once our king and his guards have now been reduced to a single foot left swimming in blood. An unknown winged creature continues to shred and chew on what looks like a leg bone. His teeth glistening in the blood, his smile cruel as we watch his stomach undulate with something live inside. Shadows of faces and hands stretch the skin across his stomach as the victims inside shout out for freedom. The sounds of bones crunching bring us out of our stupor as the stranger speaks.

"You will bow to your new king. The keep and this kingdom now belong to the Underlord."

Other creatures enter the throne room, vile, wicked, sickening, and despicable. All part of the new Underlord's minions. His pawn in the game he just won.

The creature I have in my grip struggles to speak, which is exactly why I had his tongue removed as to not alert the others. My anger at the Underlord and his reign of destruction and subjugation of the people in the wasteland fuels me forward. I drag the king's minion behind me as we continue to the other side of the keep.

This place contains two jailers who clean up the underground, but this isn't a job for the Grapner, no. She may take too long to eliminate him and he might escape to alert the king. The gurgle sounds coming out of his mouth fuels the fire inside of me, the one the king has ignited. I, too, thirst for blood and retribution.

The path towards the lower cavern is damp and smells of decay, the scent only getting stronger the farther down the steps we go. It was once a dungeon. But at the rate at which the king eliminates his people, the cells begin to remain empty, empty except for the Snare. This creature has been here since the previous king, pacing the underground for centuries, waiting to be fed.

His gaping maw, split down the center to allow his jaws to expand, swallows anything thrown at him while those punished are trapped within his belly, made from the bars of what was once our dungeon prisons. The prisoners slowly decay inside him as he continues his pacing to and fro in the bowels of this keep. A sentinel with only one mission in mind to devour all in his path. The spinal cord whip he carries in his hand can be heard dragging along the stony ground, warning those who are nearby of his arrival.

Halfway down the steps, I toss the male I have in my grip and listen as his body crashes along the rest of the descending stairs before he lands with a wet *thump*. The rumbling sound of the Snare's heavy footsteps coming towards his new meal is accompanied by the stench of death.

The gurgles become louder and then are silenced; the moans coming back again once the king's minion has been swallowed whole. Heavy footsteps continue its walk along the dungeon caverns.

Turning around, I make my way back to the barracks to prepare Khez for his journey out the back of the keep.

It is time.

ERICE

I watch as the commander exits the lower levels of the castle. He's been an interesting one to watch. I don't know his exact plans with the internal affairs, but the shrill cry of Kinsey screaming made my feet carry me further and further towards the sound.

She's here. She's close. I can feel it. But damn if it doesn't seem like the hallways rearrange themselves the longer I venture inwards. Is it a slight of mind?

Standing at the doorway that leads to what smells like a death chamber, I watch as the castle's undertaker drags a spinal whip behind him. The gurgle sounds of the creature he just devoured echo along the walls as his little hands reach out beyond the bars that line the gut. His oversized legs create a vibration with every step he takes.

I am confident Kinsey would not be found here. She's too precious a female to be tossed aside. No, the king would keep her close to play with. That's what I would do, after all.

Keeping my body within the shadows of the keep, I creep along the walls, looking for secret tunnels and doors. There has to be many since these hallways keep moving, I am sure of it! The sounds of moans and suffering are carrying into the empty corridors. What is this?

Slipping into an unlatched door along the wall, I continue to fumble into the darkness until the glow of another doorway catches my eye. Slowly, as to not make any unnecessary sounds, my feet guide me to it. With a couple of fingers, I pull the secret door back just enough to peer through.

It looks to be a bedroom. Cages hung and cages on the ground practically litter the entire space. The longer I stare, the more I realize each cage houses a female of sorts. But they are so starved, withered, and broken that one would never realize it at first glance. Is this what the Underlord has in store for my little bit? I will destroy him myself before I let that happen. I need to continue to recon this keep, find out where he's keeping her and come up with a plan that will allow us to escape with all our limbs intact.

A female's arm drops to the ground, the skin sloughing off between the metal grates as I slowly close the hidden door back to its original position.

CHAPTER
TWENTY-NINE

ISRA

Khez has arrived with the signal. A single arrow shot right into the heart of our camp. What the hell took them so long? It's been days.

My heart is racing for what Kinsey must be going through. We need to breach the keep from the back and we need to do it now! The men gathering their supplies and weapons aren't moving fast enough. Don't they understand what's at stake here? Of course, they don't because they don't understand what it's like to crave something so deeply. To want to keep that something safe and unharmed. Just the thought of her suffering is making me want to rip my own heart out.

Mentally making a decision, I charge down towards the gaping mouth of the keep, my hooves digging into the ground the faster I go. The sound of the other men following close behind me starts to become further and further away as we make our way towards what may be the battle that turns the tides of the wastelands.

KINSEY

I can barely open my eyes. It's too much. Why do my eyelids feel so heavy? I feel out of control. Just stop, just stop!

"Hold her down, she's fighting too much."

"Get both of her arms, I got her legs."

"Did you get it in yet?"

Oomph.

"Shit, she almost got me in the nuts."

"It's in, it's in."

"There we go, sweetie."

"Relax. Relax."

My mind is screaming, but my lips won't move. I feel like I'm trudging murky waters, my limbs are too heavy. Everything is going in slow motion.

"Did you hear about her case..."

I awake with a scream. The scream that was lodged in my throat. My limbs are thrashing against their phantom hands. Something jumps on top of me, holding me down and I can't take it. Always hold me down!

My wrists are gripped tightly against the mattress I'm lying on and the pain in my bones starts to ground me. The hips on top of me start to ground into me too, and another type of fear spikes. I kick and scream again until a mouth covers mine.

No, no, no! I bite down on his tongue, and he laughs, continuing his invasion with a metallic tang.

A loud knock on the door moves his face away from me.

"Enter."

My eyes are shut tight as tears start to spill down my cheeks. My mouth still tastes like his blood, and I want to spit it out.

"There's been a breach into the keep. The army has been split into two groups to check the grounds. One of my soldiers just came back to inform me that the perpetrator has been found in the south hall."

"A day of fun then. Guard my pet, commander. I will return shortly once I rid the keep of these pests."

The door shuts and I turn my face to spit out the blood, wiping my lips with the sheets below me before I bring myself up to sitting. A warm chest appears behind me as strong arms are banded around my waist. I turn to cry into his firm chest as my mind tries to hold on to sanity. I can't do this. I just can't. The Underlord toys with me like a mouse in a trap. From the boxes and cages he throws me into, to the pits of crawling creatures of nightmares grabbing at my skin and hair. It's too much. He toys with my mind, and I can never mentally prepare for anything.

He fists my hair, bringing my head back as his mouth descends on mine. What is he doing to me? I feel like I'm about to break. I push and shove at his shoulders. But he's like an immovable fortress that surrounds me.

"Give me your pain, Kinsey. Take it out on me. You must remain strong. Let me shoulder your burden for you. We need to see this plan through. I've got you."

His mouth continues to plunder mine with the intent of

dominance, and I submit. When his kisses become too passionate, too aggressive, I bite down on his tongue as well, the taste of him flooding my mouth, erasing the taste of the king. Ruspin groans as he lays me back down onto the bed.

His mouth and tongue travel everywhere, sending paths of fire on my skin.

"We need to be quick before the king returns. Open up for me Kinsey, let me give you something to erase what he's done." He doesn't wait for my response when he pushes my legs open and starts to rub his cock against my entrance. No, the king hasn't violated me there yet instead choosing to play with me mentally until I break.

I need something to hold on to before my mind splits in two. Ruspin's strength surrounds me as he forces my legs to wrap around him. The heat of his mouth makes me gasp as he sucks on my exposed breasts.

His cock continues its quick slide up and down my lips, hitting my clit each time his body pushes against me.

"What if he finds out? He'll kill me. He'll kill you."

"You're too precious for him to kill, Kinsey. Trust me."

"I can't do this anymore, Ruspin. I'm not strong enough."

"Then take my strength. You need to make it out of here alive."

Ruspin's hips pull back and his cock slides home in one hard thrust, stretching me almost to the point of pain. But what is this little pain compared to the torture the king has put me through? Ruspin growls against my neck, against the collar the king has bestowed upon me.

The sounds of his breaths increasing as he continues to slap his hips against me, pushing me into the bed, gives me a small sense of control back. I'm choosing this. I need his strength to keep me going. I'm holding onto a thread.

"Kinsey, Kinsey."

He's panting in my ear as much as I'm panting into his.

"We need to stay strong. We need to survive this. I can't do it without you. Don't you dare quit on me. I've got you. Use me. Let it all out."

His thrusts become frantic, the sounds of our bodies slapping against each other, flesh on flesh. I'm getting wetter and wetter as he refuses to let my mind think of the day's events. The smell of sex surrounds us, and it puts me into a haze. I want this. I need this. He's the only one that can give it to me. He's the only one that understands.

His teeth bite down on my shoulder as his rhythm becomes erratic, signaling how close he is to finishing. The wet sounds we're making can't be covered, so all he can do is turn this into a quickie before we're caught.

My hand travels down my stomach until my fingers reach my clit. I need this as much as he does. I can feel my body tensing, feel it ready to explode when he decides to change the angle of his thrusts, pushing us both over the edge of no return. His mouth covers mine to swallow my cry of ecstasy as he continues to pump his cum into me with his thrusts.

Ruspin is vicious in his pounding. He's so big, it's hitting me in places that are trying to take me over the ledge too quickly. My fingers scrape the back of his head and between his shoulder blades. The feel of his muscles flexing beneath me, driving me higher and higher.

When the telltale signs of my impending climax get closer, I let my stresses go and throw my head back in a pleasure-filled cry. The fact that the king might hear it just makes it even more delicious. I can feel Ruspin get bigger, and he continues to drive me into the bed like he's in a battle he's about to win.

His mouth clamps down on my closest breast, biting it, sending a sharp pain mixed with pleasure as he finishes inside of me with a snarl. When he pulls out of me, our combined juices flow onto the sheets. The king would smell that, wouldn't he? My fear starts to creep back.

It doesn't seem like Ruspin cares as his hand starts to glide over my pussy, rubbing his cum all over my stomach like a primitive marking of territory. He stands up and continues to fist his cock, which has yet to fully come down, dragging the cum he collected in his hand and rubbing it all over my thighs.

Bending down to give me another hard and dominating kiss, he tells me in a gravelly voice, "I'll come for you. Hold on for me."

Like that, he gets up and leaves the room without looking back.

CHAPTER THIRTY

ISRA

My blade slices across the neck of the creature before me as we charge into the keep. The commander's troops have done a good job in eliminating our bigger threats as we forge our way through the lesser of the king's army. The mace in my other arm feels good as I swing it down and crush the head near my hoof, his blood splattering on my forelegs.

The carnage surrounds us, the smell of blood heavy in the air, body parts littering the ground, making my hooves slip. I need to get to Kinsey. I need to keep her safe. The clashes of metal on metal, the clink of chains. The lesser army that surrounds us is no match for those who have suffered and survived the wastelands on nothing but grit.

When we breach the back hallways, the rebellion spills into one of the open rooms. A dark shadow is cast over us as a large winged creature swoops down and grabs some of our men with his talons. The agonizing scream dies as his torn body is unceremoniously dropped near us with a wet crash.

The king has arrived, and he's out for blood. But his troops have been dwindled down.

He lands on top of Bonard, his claws around his neck as Bonard tries to stab his short sword upwards into his rib cage. But the king's skin only stretches and does not pierce through, giving him the advantage.

I roar with rage as I rush to Bonard's side while slicing minions that look to have been reanimated with the King's darkness. By the time I'm able to get within swinging distance, the king decapitates Bonard's head and tosses it to the closest rebellion soldier, knocking him backward.

When his head swings my way, I bring my forelegs up and swing my mace across his head, only to have him fly backward and swiping one of his taloned feet across my side. The wound throbs as I swing my sword hand towards his ankle, but the king is an agile beast who pulls it from my grasp as he flies towards the ceiling.

"Behind you!" Drosk's voice pulls me from my fight with the king as Bonard's reanimated corpse that's still missing its head comes to attack me. My mace smashes his torso and throws him against the keep's walls.

This takeover is starting to come to a stalemate as the amount of the king's court we take down starts to come back to life.

The commander's army joins the fray with their manpower, and it looks like Khez lets an arrow go upward toward the King, who continues to hover and watch the battle below him.

"Up!"

One of the commander's men gets down on one knee as another soldier jumps onto his clasped hands, throwing him upwards.

My mind sees it happening in slow motion as he grabs a metal arrow from his quiver and pulls his bow back, letting it loose before his descent back to the ground. My eyes didn't catch it, but the soldier was able to let loose a second arrow before he lands on the ground and rolls to his feet.

The first arrow misses, but the second pierces the King in his left-wing, making him flail downwards towards us.

Drosk, the commander, and I all run towards his trajectory only to find him grabbing onto one of the reanimated corpses, softening his fall. He leaps off the body, leaving a bloody trail behind on its flesh, and opens his jaws to devour one of the males from the rebellion next to me.

I bring my back legs up and give the king a kick with all my strength, throwing him against the wall. He groans but gets back up as the skin on his head peels back to reveal his face. His feral smile tells us he's more than happy to continue this dance with us.

KINSEY

Using the sheets, I wipe Ruspin's cum off me. I can't just stay here like a damsel in distress. The strength Ruspin has lent me is fueling my rage. I need to go; I need to go now! Especially while everyone in this castle is distracted.

Looking around the room, I try to locate something I can use as a weapon. I find nothing, nothing! My hand starts to roam the walls around the room, hoping to find a trap door. After touching three walls, my hands find something that might be a door. It doesn't budge. The gap between the wall and the door is too small for me to get a good grip. I'm getting frustrated and the feeling of hopelessness is starting to encompass my mind again. I can't stay here!

My heart stops when I hear something scratching. Where is that noise coming from? My head swivels around, but the scratching sounds close. Real close. I press my ears against the door I'm trying to pry when I hear something that makes my heart beat faster.

"Little bit, step away from the door." It's muffled, but I know that voice anywhere.

I run back towards the bed, right before the door is kicked and broken through. Erice puts his foot back down before waving the dust out of his face. I never thought I'd be so happy to see that stupid smile of his. I run and jump into his arms, our lips crashing together in our reunion.

"I knew you loved me, precious. Now come on, the battle is still going. It seems our Underlord has the power to reanimate the dead. I don't know if he's going to send any of them to come to check up on you." Erice squeezes my ass before he puts me down on my feet.

His tail swats me in the back of the leg, and I frown as I turn. There at the end of it is a swath of cloth that looks mighty familiar. Grabbing it from his tail, I shake out my old dress and put it over me as Erice grabs my hand and we head into the walls of the castle.

CHAPTER THIRTY-ONE

KINSEY

The walls are dark, and I have no idea how Erice can even see anything. One of our missed turns almost landed us near the Grapner and I had to turn Erice around before we fell off the ledge that Isra was tossed over.

The sound of battle waging is starting to get louder and louder. We're close and I'm almost afraid to see who's winning. But we need to be there for the men. We need to take down the king and end all this needless suffering. I'm not even sure if the females in the keep can be saved, but one thing at a time. One obstacle at a time.

Erice finds a trapdoor that brings us into a hallway that's not far from the room the cries of war are coming from. There are blood and body parts littered everywhere, making me almost slip and fall as we walk farther and farther down.

We reach what looks like a gothic ballroom from hell. The walls and half the creatures here are bathed in red. It darkens the room exponentially. Body parts are littered on the ground next to internal organs. Some of these bodies are reanimated and walking around like there isn't a destination in mind but to get in the way.

The king's wingspan takes up a third of the room when it flares out. My eyes zoom in on what he has under his talons. It's Isra! No!

Drosk and the commander are fighting him from both sides, but the king's wingspan is keeping them just far enough. It's like having the benefit of four arms. I turn around to ask Erice what we should do when I find that he's gone. Turning back, I see that he's jumping in front of the king with both swords swinging down. But one arm swing from the king throws him to the side, landing in a pile of broken bodies... bodies that look mighty familiar. I think I see Bonard's head nearby, staring into nothingness.

What do I do? What do I do?

Half of a reanimated corpse comes towards me, and I kick it aside as I start running around the perimeter of the room, trying to figure out something. Something metal glints enough to catch my eye. What is that?

The sound of roars, grunts, and metal clashing against metal is still echoing loudly in the room as the men try to take down the king. I have to punch and push some of the reanimated bodies that are coming at me as I dive down the ground, pushing body parts aside to find...my belt. Dammit, I thought it was going to be a knife or a sword. My hand grabs it anyway just as the air current starts to move my hair and I'm pulled off the ground by my dress.

We're flying higher and higher as some of the men try to figure out how to get us down. The king has me in his talons and I'm stuck between a rock and a hard place because if he opens up his claws, I will probably fall to my death.

Some of Ruspin's soldiers get down on one knee as Ruspin sprints and jumps off their backs right for me. Both of his arms have shifted into blades as he prepares to swing them inwards to cut off the king's legs.

"Nooooo!" My screech carries enough for Ruspin to stop mid-swing, allowing the king to beat one of his wings against him, plummeting him downwards. NO! I didn't mean for that to happen! Instead of me falling to my death, it's Ruspin!

His men move quickly to create a sort of forearm barrier that Ruspin lands on, toppling his men over. But at least no one is dead.

I'm so distracted by what's happening below us that I didn't catch the king bringing his leg up and throwing me over his shoulder to ride him as he flies out of the ballroom of death. I almost fall off his back when I realize I'm still holding onto my belt.

I don't think I just act as I swing the belt around his neck and pull tight with both hands. The king starts to choke and flail. We run into walls as we fall towards the ground. Both of my arms are still holding tight as the king crashes right on top of me on a pile of bodies, knocking the wind out of me.

Erice jumps onto the king right at that moment, pushing his weight further into me and knocking even more breath out of my lungs. The glint of his blades slashing across the king's neck becomes overshadowed by the roar that vibrates through my very body.

Ruspin grabs me under my arms and pulls me out from beneath the king, throwing me towards another body that lifts me up. The smell of Isra and blood seep into my nose, but it doesn't stop me from wrapping my arms around his neck. As Isra moves away from the battle scene, I chance a peek back and see both Erice and Ruspin slashing into the king like the future of this world depends on it. In a way, I guess it does.

Erice and Ruspin growl and roar as Erice slices into one of the King's wings, eliciting a cry of agony from his lips.

Ruspin drives the final blow into the Underlord's chest again and again, the blood splattering all over his chest and face, but it doesn't stop his rage. When the King takes his final breath, Ruspin decapitates him and screams into the head in his grip.

"Down with the tyrant king!" What's left of the commander's troops and the rebellion cheer and repeat the mantra as I turn to bury my head into Isra's shoulder to muffle the sound. I'm so damn tired, and now that the battle's won...I can finally find peace and rest.

"Isra, the females."

"What do you speak of?"

"There are females kept in cages in the Underlord's bed chambers. We need to free them."

"Little bit, you are the only female here."

"What do you mean? There are other females kept in cages everywhere inside of cages scattered in the King's bedchamber!"

"Shh..shhh.. Kinsey. Kinsey! You're dreaming. Wake up."

"What?"

"Open your eyes, Kinsey, there's no one here but you. *Open your eyes.*"

CHAPTER THIRTY-TWO

WAYLON

The process it took for me to become Kinsey's conservator took longer than I'd like. Grandmother was admitted into a nursing home about a year before the murder of our father. I'm all she has left. Something snapped in her that fateful day. I can't let her down.

Once the judge appointed me, I did everything I could to remove her from the institution they threw her in. Fucking bastards. When I read over what they were doing to her, I was fucking livid. She's been thrown into a straight-jacket, tied down in her bed, and forced a cocktail of medications to make her more 'compliant'. The amount of 'cocktails' they had to give her over a short period of time is abhorrent.

They never did find David.

She's been transferred to three facilities so far. This one was meant to be the last stop. Well, it's going to be now that I'm here. This shit ends now.

Walking around the hallways, I can understand why they

take the precautious road. Almost everyone here is off their rockers. The sterile walls, the cold temperature, and grey carpet only add to the insanity one might find here. I'd go crazy too, staring at this all day. Half the people here walk like zombies from too many meds and who knows what else.

Is this what Kinsey had to go through? *My god.* My blood boils at the thought.

"You fucking cut my head off last night! I know it was you, you bastard!" One of the patients jumps on the orderly and proceeds to start throwing fists. Three other orderlies run towards the fight, tackling the guy down before a needle is shoved into his inner elbow. He's dragged away as a nurse comes to check on the orderly on the ground.

This place is a fucking zoo. My steps quicken towards room 301, Kinsey's room. When I make it to the front of the door, I knock before I let myself inside.

Hair is brushed to the side of the pillow. Her eyes are staring at the wall. The closer I get, the more enraged I get when I see her wrists tied down to the bed. Fuck!

There's a chair in the corner, so I drag it to the side of her bed. Sitting down, I put my hands on hers and speak out loud, hoping she can hear me.

"Kinsey. Kinsey. I'm so fucking sorry."

She thrashes, but her body can't move much from being tied down. Her legs are kicking and scissoring. I run out the door to her room and yell for a nurse before running back to the chair beside her. All they have on her is a damn hospital gown in the front and back. Where the fuck are her clothes?

"Kinsey! Kinsey! It's just me. You're the only one here. Wake up, Kinsey!" My hand caresses her cheek as I lean in right before I speak into her ear. "It's just me and you, Kinsey. Open your eyes. Come on baby, open your eyes."

Her eyes flutter and tears are starting to stream down to the pillow. It breaks my fucking heart and I feel like breaking someone's neck. When the nurse gets here, she checks over Kinsey's vitals and monitors her heartrate.

"She has medication PRN. Would you like me to administer it?"

"No." I don't give a fuck what they've been giving her to 'help her' because obviously, it isn't. This isn't the Kinsey I know. This person is a shadow of who she is, lost in the darkness of her mind. She's had nightmares before, but not like this. She needs to detox from whatever the fuck they've been injecting her with. It's probably making her worse instead of better.

The nurse nods and takes off the pulse oximeter from her finger, then proceeds to leave the room. I continue to caress the side of her face and she starts to settle back down, eyes closed. Dammit, Kinsey, what have they been doing to you here?

KINSEY IS MORE LUCID TODAY. I'VE BEEN COMING IN TO SEE HER every day for about a week. She cried when she saw me, making my chest hurt. When she buried her face in my chest and hugged me, my heart broke. I need to get her out of this crazy place. We've been weaning her off some of her meds and I've been continuously talking to the case manager about her progress.

I need to bring her home. These fuckers don't get it. She needs to come home now.

"Waylon. I've missed you. Please take me home. I can't remember myself here. I can't remember anything but the hands. Waylon, please!"

I cradle her face into my chest again as we both sit on her bed. She's become so fragile; it hurts me to watch her like this. It angers me that I can't just bash someone's face in without harsh repercussions to her leaving this place.

"David!" I grind my teeth as I watch her jump into his arms. They've become closer and closer these past few years. He doesn't deserve her. She's mine to protect. She's been through enough in her life to crush on a guy like David who's been around the block twice. Friend or not, Kinsey is my sister, dammit.

I grab the back of his collar and pry him off her. My growth spurt has given me a one-up on the height aspect between us. My father sending me out to fight for cash and to deal on the streets has made me more reckless. I know it, but I'd lay my life down for my sister. Fuck this fool right here, right now. If I had to choose, I'd choose Kinsey every time.

"Get off my sister, fucker. I ain't going to tell you twice." I shove his shoulders so hard he almost falls. Good. Then Kinsey can see how weak he is. He's not strong enough to be her man. Not with all the shit we go through at home. I'll always be there for her. I don't trust this jackass one bit with the way he's been trying to slither into her life.

"Kinsey, I'mma get you home soon. I promise. Hold on for me. I'll come back for you, I swear it." I kiss her on the cheek before I walk out of her room and demand another meeting with the case manager, behavioral specialist, and whatever other services this place provides. I'm not leaving my damn sister in this madhouse. She's safer with me. I've seen the way the orderlies look at her here, and the other patients. I know my sister's exotic features make her a novelty. It's the same look David always gave her when he thought I wasn't looking.

Fuck this place.

I've missed her stormy grey eyes. I need to bring her home so we can visit our grandmother in the nursing home now that my father is out of the picture. Now that we're finally safe.

CHAPTER THIRTY-THREE

KINSEY

"Come back to me, little bit. I've missed you." His lips cover mine and I can't even answer him, but I've *fucking missed him too.*

My eyes flutter, and I can't seem to get back to where I've once been.

"My dark queen, I would have laid my life down for you." I know you would have Isra. Fuck, I've missed you.

"You smell of different males and it drives me to bloodlust, Kinsey." Ruspin thrusts into me harder and harder, driving me over the cliff of pleasure. How does he do that? How does he dominate me so and make me want to submit so easily?

The dual swords appear across his neck as he smiles menacingly and continues to pound into my wet pussy, not even caring one bit. I want him so bad; I want his strength and his dominance to keep me safe.

The swords disappear, and it's just me and Ruspin. The feel of him, his heat, the friction between our bodies. At certain angles, he feels too big for me. His aura surrounds us, not letting me give him no for an answer, not that I'd ever want to. The glide of his cock as it goes in and out amplifies my already sensitive insides, making me climb and climb towards the point of no return. When I think I can't take any more of his hips grinding against my clit, his hand circles the back of my neck, forcing me to kiss him and duel with our tongues. He knows he'll always win the battle. He knows I'll always submit to him, knowing he'd fight to win for me.

I awake with a start and when my eyes fully open; I peer into hazel ones. Ones that melt my insides. Ones that bring me comfort.

I jump out of the bed and feel surprised when my hands aren't restrained today, throwing my arms around his neck. Waylon smells of home, he smells of safety. My anchor to reality when I feel like I'm going to lose my damn mind. Some days I can't tell what's real and what's not. A continuous prisoner, whether my eyes are open or closed.

"Don't cry, baby, I'm going to get you out of here. The case management meeting told me you'll be out by this week. Just hold on and survive okay. I give you my word I'll come back for you. Trust me." I rub my tear-stained face against his chest and hold on tighter. I don't know how much longer I can survive this before I start to lose myself.

His hugs are so warm, so real. I'm afraid to let go.

As he rubs his warm palm against my back, I'm reminded of the men I left behind in my nightmares.

"Kinsey, I need to go. I need to sort out this process of bringing you home, the final run around they're giving me." He pets my hair and cradles my face. "I promise I'll get you out of here. Trust me." With a chaste kiss on the forehead, he walks out of the room.

It seems Waylon brought some clothes for me today because there's a pile of folded clothes on the chair in the corner of the room. How long have I been in this gown? I quickly get up to change to find some sort of semblance of normalcy. Running my hands down my clothes, I take a deep breath and decide to take on the day. Exiting the safety of my room is scary. I don't know what I'll find out there. Then again, look at what they've been doing to me in here.

Erice, Isra, Ruspin. The rebellion. My mind is still in a haze of images that start to fade like images in the rain the more steps I take. I didn't think we would survive it, the bloodshed and carnage, but we did. They made me hold on, kept my sanity in check, as I was constantly put under with liquid restraint.

Haldol, Benadryl and Ativan. Who knew a small cocktail would make me 'compliant'. I was a walking zombie. Everything is a haze, and I can't even remember being upright. Wandering the halls to find refuge, but only finding a different kind of restraint. I don't have any memories of what I've done. Or maybe I do? Bits and pieces. Other psychotropics they put in me made me barely able to catch a breath, as my mind felt like it was drowning in a raging ocean. Mental waves that continue to crash down on me, pulling me more and more into the dark depths of the sea. I was lost in the nightmares, lost in my mind.

From liquid restraint to physical restraint, I was lost in the chaos. The veil of reality and subconsciousness was wearing thin, leaking like blood spreading into my nightmares, coating the world in red and umbers. The moss, the cracked dirt, the red of the beasts that fill the skies.

Here. Here I'm surrounded by whites and greys. The metals of rails on the side of the hallways, cold to the touch. The only splashes of life of color coming from the light tan of the orderlies' scrubs. Everyone's eyes hide darkness under the facade of beauty and smiles. The nurses are happy to give you your medicine as one of the orderlies finger sweep your mouth, like a sexual torture, to make sure everything they've given you has been swallowed.

"Swallow it all. That's a good girl."

The pictures that line the walls are of places that don't exist. They're too happy to exist. Whoever painted them must have drudged up memories from dreams to have colors like that. But against the sterile environment that surrounds us, there is a dull cast over the pictures like this place wants to swallow it whole too.

I'm walking down the hall with some others. At least this time I remember doing it. I'm slowly going insane with the flashes in my mind. Pieces to the puzzle that just can't seem to fit. I shake my head and try to dislodge it, or at least try to shuffle the pieces and make it fit better. Fuck, I can't even trust my mind anymore.

The blood splatters the walls, my hands all over my face. The warmth of it cooling quickly with each breath I take. Streaks of crimson everywhere, all over my shirt, everywhere I look. My world's been painted in red.

The longer I cry, the more I notice the contrast in temperature between the two on my face. The cooling blood. The warm tears flowing down my face. What the fuck?! It's over, but it's only begun.

My hand is holding something. It's heavy, it's grounding me. I'm in a zone. Blinking a few times, I hear my brother Waylon growl. Turning to my right, I watch as the blood drips from his chin and I can't help but feel so calm...so relieved. It's done. It's finally done. He won't hurt us anymore.

I'm still staring into his eyes as the body beneath us lets out a crackling, wet breath one last time before everything falls quiet around us.

I did it, didn't I? I killed our father. That wretched soul that devours anyone who comes near him. He can't hurt us anymore. That's something I hold on to.

I want to go home. I can't stand this place.

They don't tackle me anymore. The constriction and pain from the straight jacket they used to lace around me. I thought it was a dream, but Waylon told me the truth. Becoming my conservator allowed him to view my medical records. I don't care if killing our father was wrong. This fucking place did me wrong!

I watch as the orderly next to me takes down a patient who screams.

"You fuckers right here, all work for the fucking King. He puts us in these cages and plays with our minds. I'm fucking onto you all! You all keep us down and make us think we're crazy when it's all of you who are crazy!! None of this is real!"

His menacing smile is directed at me when two of the orderlies tackle him to the ground and he's injected with a concoction that calms him down. A personal cocktail that makes him more pliant to their requests.

All the other patients, including myself, stare onward without a sound, watching everything unfold like it's just another day. Because it really is just another day. Some of the patients in the rooms next to me were transferred from the prison for the criminally insane. They haven't come out of their haze yet, barely leaving their rooms, barely moving a muscle.

One guy is tall, dark, and brooding. His shoulders are so wide it looks like he's wearing armor when in reality they're just his natural trap muscles. He always gives me a tender smile when I walk by, and I don't know what to think of it.

At lunch, I see the guy they tackled down earlier. He's been released, and he's zoning out, staring into the walls as he mechanically chews his food like he doesn't taste it. When his eyes suddenly swing to me, his smile reminds me of a shark waiting for its prey to slip into the waters.

I turn my head around to watch one of the orderlies stare at me. Was he looking at me this whole time? Why? Something about his commanding presence makes me submit my eyes and turn my gaze back to my plate. I barely taste what I'm chewing. Who knows what they're feeding us. My nose tells me it smells decent.

This place is going to drive me insane if it hasn't already. Waylon made them taper down the meds and my mind is just starting to clear the fog that always hangs around. I can't help but feel like I'm missing something, I'm missing some part of myself.

When I asked to see my chart, my patient history states that I've been charged with aiding in the murder of my father with an insanity defense. Is that so? I remember the blood; I remember the warmth of it dripping down my face as it started to cool the longer I stood over the body.

My mind must have blanked out and protected me

because everything is fragmented. Pieces of the puzzle that have no full picture to refer to.

Raising my head again, the orderly's eyes sharpen, and his smile starts to freak me out. But when I turn, all I see are piranha teeth. On the other side are sets of eyes that soften as they gaze upon me like he wishes to protect me from the horrors of this place.

But that's not true. No one can.

We're all in this hellhole together, stuck in the different layers of hell. Half of us know where we are, half of us wander the halls like reanimated corpses.

CHAPTER THIRTY-FOUR

WAYLON

Today's the day I bring Kinsey home. Fucking finally. These bastards don't make it easy, despite giving you the initial yes for Conservatorship.

Well, today is going to be a *fuck you* to this place and everyone in it. A *fuck you* to everyone who did my Kinsey wrong.

She doesn't have much to pack since she's been in a damn hospital gown the majority of her stay here. At least she has the clothes I brought her the other day. As I walk with her to her room to do a final sweep, some of the patients here are looking at me strangely.

Well, not so strangely. More like they hate the fact that I'm taking her out of this place. *Fuck you all.* There's one orderly who's been giving me a hard time trying to throw his authority around. I have a fucking feeling that he wants Kinsey to stay for his own purposes.

When I finally bring Kinsey beyond the double-gated exit

door, she stops and lifts her face to the sky to take a deep breath in and out. My heart constricts and my anger rises. Gently putting my hand on her lower back, we both move towards the car I have parked nearby.

The drive back to town was slow and quiet. Kinsey hasn't said much since we left. Please don't tell me she's already become institutionalized. It took me a fucking year to get her out with everything that's happened.

"Is Grandmother alright?" It sounds louder than it is because it's the first thing she said since getting in the car.

"Yea, they're taking care of her well." She nods and doesn't say anything else. What's going on in that mind of yours, Kinsey?

We drive for thirty more minutes before stopping. Kinsey peers out the window with a frown. "Where are we?"

"I got an apartment in a different city." She nods again, trusting I know what I'm doing.

Opening the passenger door for her, I escort her up a couple of flights of stairs until we reach our apartment door. She's hesitant when she looks back at me, but I give her a soft smile and she continues to place one foot in front of the other before entering the living room.

I encouraged Kinsey to take a shower in case it helps to liven her spirits up. She comes out in one of my t-shirts with her hair still dripping wet and it's a sight I've missed. Kinsey relaxed and almost content.

We order pizza and as Kinsey is chewing, watching TV, and sitting between my legs, using me as a backrest. She hasn't stopped finding opportunities to physically touch me since we came 'home'. My mind is going nuts trying to figure out the horrors she must have been through to make her so starved for touch this way. Leaning back a little, I grab the packet of paperwork they gave me when we left. I go over her list of medications again. They have her on so much shit, I'm surprised she can even respond to me correctly. I need to get her off this stuff.

Once we're done eating, Kinsey helps me clean up. I lead her to the bedroom and watch her reaction. She hasn't let go of my hand yet.

I tell her to lie down and take a nap while I rearrange some of the closet space to make room for her things. Since the incident with our father, I was only able to grab some of her stuff and bring it in my move to this apartment. It's still in boxes and I have yet to hang them up. By the time I get ready for bed, Kinsey is already fast asleep. Careful as to not wake her, I slide in behind her and hold her close to me, feeling the weight on my shoulders lifted now that I have her back and safe.

CHAPTER THIRTY-FIVE

KINSEY

Reflections.

Is it a mirror? It's wavering for a minute but then calms.

What I thought was me stretches and contracts until...it's just me I'm seeing, with a smile.

Fangs. Rows of them. Elongate before my very eyes. There they are.

A tail slides up my ankle and thigh as his smile gets even wider right before he kisses me behind the neck.

"Hello, precious." Who would have thought I'd miss this bastard and his pet names?

He's tossed aside and all I can hear is his booming laugh as Ruspin forces me around for a hard and dominant kiss. I barely catch my breath when he pulls away and the air around him feels stifling from his commanding presence. He rubs his face over my cheek as his hands roam my waist and hips with a sense of ownership.

"The knight has two minutes. Then your time is mine." Always so commanding.

He sidesteps and I'm lifted into warm arms. My own arms go around his neck to prevent me from falling.

"My dark queen. You're alive and well. I've missed you." Oh, Isra. Always the gentleman.

"I've missed you t-.."

"Your time is up, Knight." What an asshole, it's only been like five seconds.

"Yes, my King." Wait, what? I turn to catch his menacing smile as he crosses his arms over his broad chest, emphasizing his physique. The scrollwork on his body glowing more than I remember. Ruspin? Isra puts me down on my feet and I'm hauled against Ruspin's hard chest.

"What would you do for your king, little female?" His voice is lowered, husky and somehow everyone's disappeared but us. His hot breath tickling my ear and the crook of my neck.

"I don't need to do a damn thing for you Ruspin, and you know it. I've done enough." Do I sound out of breath? His presence is always so damn overwhelming to my senses. He chuckles as he lowers himself to one knee and spreads my legs apart with a firm grip. His tongue leaves a wet trail along my lower belly and my breathing picks up even more. What is he planning to do? His calloused hands are doing things to my lady bits.

"I plan to conquer you, starting with this spanse of land right here..." The hot tongue that enters my pussy almost makes my knees buckle from the pleasure.

I'm squirming and opening my legs up even wider at the same time. His hot breath touches my skin and I feel the goosebumps rising. My hand automatically goes to the back of his head, pulling him in, silently asking for more of what he's giving me.

When his tongue circles my clit, and a finger enters my pussy, I moan. Shit, that feels so good. Another finger and another. When he takes it out, I almost whimper in protest until he invades my pussy with his tongue again. My arms cross over my face as my hips try to push the tongue deeper. A soft chuckle sends vibrations on my lower lips, making me gasp quietly.

The body starts climbing mine, peppering soft kisses along the way until he reaches my right breast. His hot mouth takes my entire areola and nipple in while his other hands softly knead my other breast, giving it equal amounts of attention. His hips are slowly flexing against my leg, and I can feel his hardness against me, teasing me with what I want.

I grab his face with both my hands and bring him up to my lips so I can devour his wicked tongue with mine, aligning us for what we both want and need. He groans into my mouth and the sound is lost as I swallow it down, our lips and tongues fighting for something. Something we've both missed.

Emboldened and hungry. My hand shoots down and grabs a firm hold on his cock, stroking it between our bodies, eliciting another groan from his mouth. I like this control I have over him. I like making him *mine*.

Rubbing his cock along my wet slit, I tease myself around my clit and channel with just an inch of him. Both of our breathing is picking up, making the room feel hotter than it is. His face goes to the crook of my neck, and I can feel him sucking against my skin. More, I want more. I need to feel more. Knowing he's marking me makes me burn from the inside.

His hands force mine away from his cock and I almost scream in protest as he cages both my wrists on either side of my head and shoves it into me with one hard thrust. The fullness and the stretch give me just enough pain to ground me, making me feel alive. It's been so long; I feel like a virgin all over again.

"Shit, Kinsey. You're so fucking tight." And you love it.

His hips start slapping mine with a ferocity of a feral animal as I bring my hips up to match his cadence. I need him deeper in me. I need him to fill the holes I feel inside my soul. I'm getting wetter and wetter, and this fire inside of me is burning hotter and hotter.

When he pushes the back of one of my knees up and out and changes the angle of his thrust, my body starts to tense up in anticipation. His speed hasn't died down one bit, his sweat trickling down between his pecs and abs as his muscle continues to strain with his invasion. He means to conquer me. I lick a bead of sweat I find coming down the cord of his neck and nip at his skin, telling him I want it harder; I want his madness to fill me up. I love him dominating my body like this.

His lips find mine again and we're kissing so hard our teeth are hitting each other now and again. I fucking love it. My hand lowers and finds my clit, rubbing circles as we continue this battle of wills with our lips and tongues. I bite his lower lip hard enough for him to bleed and greedily lick it up, sharing the metallic taste with him. He growls and his hips become erratic, losing its rhythm. He feels like he's getting bigger and with one hard thrust to the hilt, his body vibrates as he groans into the crook of my neck, right beside my ear. I love that I can do that to him. I love that when he dominates me, he also surrenders to me.

"You're so fucking precious to me."

Though his thrusts have slowed down, continually shooting his cum in me, my fingers have not stopped moving. The sensations are getting higher and higher and I fall off the mental cliff as he pushes a finger in my ass, invading my tight ring of muscle.

"Ahhh..." My cries of ecstasy are cut short when his mouth covers mine in a much softer, much more loving lip lock. We continue our slow kiss as he removes his finger and his cock slides out of me, our combined juices wetting my inner thighs.

With one last chaste peck, Waylon gets up in the dark and goes to the restroom to wash. He comes back with a wet cloth and cleans me tenderly between my legs, kissing the inside of my thighs every now and again. Tossing the rag into the laundry hamper, he spoons behind me and nuzzles my hair, breathing me in, as we slowly drift back off to sleep.

WAYLON

Fuck, I've missed her. I've missed this. She's all I have. All we have is each other. I fucking love her, down to the depths of my soul. She's the other half of me.

Listening to the sound of her breathing slowly as she falls asleep is the best thing in the world and I'm never letting her go ever again.

That fucker David has been all up at my sister these days. I know he wants to fuck her. I can see it in his eyes. My mind sees red and I'm imagining all the ways I can dismember him and hide the evidence. She's mine!

The sound of my sister's laughter drifts to where I'm standing, hidden behind the back of the house. I love her laugh. It fills my soul. But her laugh belongs to me and only me. I'm going to fucking kill him in his sleep.

My eyes start to feel heavy as I find myself drifting off into the darkness with Kinsey in my arms. The scent of her, my kryptonite. It's so wrong, but it's so right. We're right where we both belong.

The rage inside my mind explodes with fury when I come home from one of our father's stupid errands and find him on top of Kinsey through the side window. She's crying and my fists ball up as I race to the front of the house as fast as my feet can carry me.

I hear David's voice and he better not be fucking here to violate her, either. I'm going to kill them both!

"Kinsey! Get the fuck off her!" I know what I heard, but my mind is still telling me to make them pay. Make them all pay for the shit they've put us through.

"Get out of my house, boy. You have no business here. If I catch you in my house again, I will cut you limb from limb and spread it out over the city so your mother will never find you." The venom in his voice drips into me, poisoning me with his darkness. Like father, like son.

By the time I make it to the porch, the sound of my father dragging a body to the back becomes the only thing I hear.

When our father comes back to our room to finish what he started with Kinsey, I run quickly to the kitchen to grab a knife and finally do what I've always been meant to do. Kinsey is mine*! I'm the only one that can save her from this wretched creature we call our father. This King of nothing. My entire being becomes consumed with one mission and one mission alone.*

The blade comes down on his back. When he turns to look me dead in the eye, I pull the blade out and slash him across his throat, his blood spraying all over me like a baptism.

I smile as his face starts to register the truth. I laugh out loud because what does this fucker know about truth? He hides his debauchery within the walls we call home. My hand comes down again and again, making sure to release all the darkness he has inside of him. To rid the world of demons and nightmares like him. The blade slices easier and easier with each swing I bring down. I'm in a haze, muscle memory, I can't stop. I can hear Kinsey scrambling in the room to grab something, but my mind is focused on the task at hand.

Only when his stomach is gaping, exposing his innards like hamburger meat, does my rage start to simmer. My heart is beating wildly. I feel fucking primal. I step over the corpse and grab Kinsey for a branding kiss, smearing her face in crimson like a blood pact. No one is going to stand in my way again. No one is going to separate us. The only person Kinsey needs is me. I will always protect her, no matter what it takes.

My mind goes back to David. The fucker knows too much. Releasing Kinsey, I march to the back of the house to find him on the ground, still breathing. Dragging him back into the house, I make sure to color him up with the red we've painted. Placing the knife in his hand, I give Kinsey a final kiss before telling her what she needs to do.

"I was never here, Kinsey. David and our father had an altercation. He came upon our father raping you and towards the end

of the fight, David killed him. You understand me?" She nods, her eyes full of tears and trust. Fuck, she is beautiful when she cries. "I promise you, I will come for you, Kinsey. You have my word. But you gotta see the plan through. Endure until I get there."

When she nods in understanding, the admiration glinting in her eyes, I run out the back of the house. Does that make me a bastard? I had to. It was the only way so that I could rescue her later. What good would I be to get caught with her?

My thoughts start to drift to the weight of David's body as I chuck pieces of him down the river, right before the darkness of sleep and the smell of Kinsey consumes me.

PLAYLIST

Within Temptation - The Dance
Evanescence - Sweet Sacrifice
Flyleaf - Sick
Within Temptation - The Gatekeeper
Collide - Transfer
Otep - Buried Alive
Kittie - Charlotte
Metallica - King Nothing
Cradle of Filth - Temptation
Theater of Tragedy - Venus
Evanescence - A New Way to Bleed
After Forever - Energize Me
Kittie - What I Always Wanted
Within Temptation - Over The Hills

If you get your kicks in a magical manner, order toys from websites like bad dragon, and prefer your monsters *in* your bed instead of *under* them, then Y. D. is your girl.

Writing everything from spicy dark fantasy to fluffier-than-a-cool-marshmallow romance, Y.D. La Mar has her fingers in all sorts of man-meat pie, and the sky is the limit. Somehow, this magical mistress manages to balance her spicy author life with her responsibilities as a mom, a wife, and a resident of Sin City—*oh, irony, you've felled me.*

When the world is full of black-and-white, Y.D. plays in the grey zones, spending her time creating new ways to shock and awe her editor, as well as her readers.

Follow Me!

WANT UPDATES AND SNEAK PEEKS?

Sign up for my newsletter!

ALSO BY YD LA MAR

STREET ARRHYTHMIA TRILOGY

The Scent of Jasmine

For The Love of Import & Blood

To The Beat of The Streets

Spinoff

Arachnophilia

REVERSE HAREM

Warring Suns

SCI FI

The Essence of Esme

PARANORMAL

The Hunger of Thieves

Heart of The Reaper

Heart of the Reaper: Tales from the Underworld

Soul of The Reaper

Fate of The Reaper

Bury Me Alive

Lead Me Through The Fire

PSYCHOLOGICAL THRILLER

The Truth Enslaved

CONTEMPORARY

The Formation of Us

The Conception of Us

The Revelation of Us

The House of Eden (cowrite)

When the Bloom Burns (cowrite)

OMEGAVERSE

Gero

Bernhard

Severin

DYSTOPIAN/POST APOCALYPTIC

We Are the Fallen

MONSTER SHORT STORIES

Sinful Attraction

The Sky Below

Maeonia

Between Heaven and Earth

Fantasies Inflamed

Her 13th Hour

Ignus Fatuus

ANTHOLOGIES

Used and Bound

Captured by Darkness

Until the End

After the Rain

Into The Woods

A Foster Fling

Bound by Monsters

Once Upon a Nightmare

Monsters in Love: Lost in the Dark

Monsters in Love: Lost in the Forest

Monsters in Love: Monstrous Ever After

Monsters in Love: Lost in the Deeps

Monsters in Love: Aloha Nui Loa

Pollinators

The Red Key Club: Valentines Day Edition

The Red Key Club: Halloween Edition

Creepy Court

Crimson Vendetta

For the Love of Villains

SHARED WORLDS

Inferno World

Games of the Underworld

Rise of the Dreads

Monsters Ball

Rescue Me: A Hero Romance Collection

HEART OF THE REAPER

BLURB

My dark past was only a foreshadowing of my future.

Once an ordinary girl, my life was forever altered when those I trusted the most gave into their dark desires. I was cast into the underworld, but I didn't belong there.

And he knew it.

The Reaper, the formidable ruler of this realm, spared me, sending me back to a human world I no longer recognized.

I should have been grateful, but instead, I found myself missing the one who cast me out. And I wasn't the only one grappling with unexpected longing. The Reaper himself, against all reason, yearned for me. Consumed by this unfamiliar desire, he waged wars, devoured souls, and defied his nature, just to take a corporeal form and win my heart.

But can a mortal woman truly love Death? And what happens when the heart I hold in my hands is the most dangerous thing of all?

Courtesy warning: This book may contain triggers for some. Triggers include but are not limited to non-con, unrequited family love, dub-con, knife play, suicidal ideation, depression, violence, blood play, BDSM, choking, biting, demons devouring human flesh, humans devouring demon flesh, themes of war and human trafficking, torture, themes that may be disturbing to some readers.

HEART OF THE REAPER

www.ingramcontent.com/pod-product-compliance
Lightning Source LLC
Chambersburg PA
CBHW071415200726
48294CB00002B/408

* 9 7 8 1 9 6 2 4 0 3 1 8 4 *